The Lost Art
of
Fishing Stories

The Lost Art of Fishing Stories

Written by
Andrew J. Cox

Illustrations by
Onie "Virginia" Bailey

Copyright © 2023 Andrew J. Cox

All rights reserved. No part of this book may be reproduced or used in any manner without the prior written permission of the copyright owner, except for the use of brief quotations in a book review.

To request permissions or if you have questions please contact the publisher at coxfamilypublishers@gmail.com.

Paperback: ISBN: 979-8-9893854-0-9
Ebook: ISBN: 979-8-9893854-1-6

First paperback edition November 2023.

Cover Art by Onie "Virginia" Bailey
Illustrations by Onie "Virginia" Bailey
Photographs owned by Andrew J. Cox
Edited by Cox Family Publishers

Dedication

Dedicated to my wonderful wife, Karleen Cox, who has supported me in every adventure and to my beautiful daughters, Maddie Jean Starr and Tayla Jo Allyson, who keeps me young at heart every day.

If I fished only to capture fish, my fishing trips would have ended long ago.

ZANE GREY

Contents

Introduction……………………………………………....11

Story 1: The Lost Art …………………………………..15

Story 2: Surf Fishing ……………………………….......35

Story 3: Like a Pro ……………………………………...51

Story 4: Big Man Upstairs ……………………………...69

Story 5: Secret Honey Hole ………………...………….75

Story 6: Words of Wisdom ………………………….....95

Story 7: Bamboo Heritage ……………………………..103

About the Author ……………………………………...135

About the Illustrator …………………...……….……...137

Introduction

My fly fishing started much later in life than most. I was in my 30's before I even attempted to fly fish. Once I started this sport, I quickly realized that fly fishing is a "lost art" and through trial and error I slowly learned this "lost art" to at least an amateur level. During my long hours spent learning to cast, tie flies, and attempt to catch fish (not very successful starting out) I had many thoughts about life and growing up learning "lost arts" that unfortunately don't get passed down to everyone. I had many conversations with myself and did some deep soul searching on each fishing trip.

I started telling my fishing stories to my friends and family and they brought up that I should write the stories down. After giving that some time to marinate, I decided that I would do just that; write my crazy stories. With that I decided to reach out to my local hometown paper (Vian Tenkiller News) to see if they would be interested in me writing a column for their paper and they agreed. This book contains some of the stories I wrote for that paper. It was a fun time writing the stories and I hope that you enjoy them as much as I did writing them.

"Wishing you bent rods and tight lines."

Story 1:
The Lost Art

The Lost Art

Beep, Beep, Beep, Beep............"Nnnnnoooo, to early!!!!"

Reminding me how early it was, my wife says, "Please turn the alarm off and go back to sleep. You know you aren't really going this early."

"It's not that I want to get up this early, but the earlier the better. Just go back to sleep."

"Whatever!"

As I try to get up, the dogs, laying between my legs, look up as if saying, "if you think I'm moving for you, you have another thing coming." So, I do the next best thing, pull my legs up toward my chest, over the dogs, and slowly sit up.

"Don't worry yourself, I can manage without your help." After sitting there for several minutes thinking maybe this is a bad idea I decide to get up and start the day.

"First things first, coffee!"

Getting up this early I know I will need something to get me going. I go into the kitchen, start a pot of coffee, knowing I need enough for my thermos as well.

THE LOST ART OF FISHING STORIES

I then stumble to the bathroom for the morning routine of the three S's. Completing the third S, I look myself in the mirror.

"It will be worth it once the day is done."

I get dressed as warm as I can. Long johns, running pants, long sleeve shirt, boots, beanie, and neck gator. This should keep me warm the rest of the morning.

I make my way over to my wife, still sleeping away.

How in the world was I able to get a woman this great?

She's followed me around the world during my Marine Corps career pushing me to do my best, reminding me that I can do anything I set my mind to. She is the perfect wife.

I lean over saying quietly, "I love you sweetie" and give her a kiss on her cheek.

She mumbles, "I love you too".

I wonder if she has just said it as a response to the morning routine. Many times, she has said,

"I don't remember when you leave in the mornings and what is said between the two of us."

I laugh out loud and head for the kitchen. When I reach the coffee pot, I fill my travel mug. As I reach over to grab my thermos a memory of my father floods over me. I remember going to work with him when I was around ten and he had an old beat-up thermos. It was green with a silver cap that served as his coffee cup. This is the reason I purchased my thermos, green with the silver cap. I guess I'm still trying to be like dad. He has been in heaven for a while and I wish we could still share time together, but what better way to communicate with him than to emulate him. They say, to emulate someone is the best form of flattery and I am still trying to emulate a great man.

After filling my thermos, I hear my father-in-law just getting up, probably taking medicine, and getting dressed for the day. Well, I may not have dad here anymore, but at least I have my father-in-law. It's great to still have that father figure. I should probably tell him, so he knows how I feel. Maybe later in the day. I do need to get on the road.

"Dang! I forgot to warm the truck up," I exclaim.

Oh well, I guess the ride there will be a little chilly. That's what I get for letting my mind wonder and not paying attention to what is going on. I get in the truck, start it, look in the mirror seeing the exhaust.

"Yep, it's cold out.! Well, here I go."

I start heading down the road, my truck revved up as it's still a little cold. The land here on the mountain is sure pretty. I have been many places; California, North Carolina, Virginia, Japan, Iraq, all the states across I-40 and I-20 from sea to shining sea; and realize that it is here, small town, Vian and Blackgum, Oklahoma, that I enjoy being the most. I drive by Lake Tenkiller and start getting a little excited. It is this lake that feeds my addiction. Yes, I said addiction. Addiction may be a little strong, but I do love it.

I continue on down the road past the lake and toward Gore. Taking this road brings back more memories. I remember visiting cousins as a child and thinking how long it took to drive the ten miles from Vian to Gore. It had to have taken a good hour and a half to get there. It always seemed like an all-day excursion to a young child. I laugh out loud.

"I guess it is true. The older you get the faster time flies."

I flash out of the memory just in time to see my turn. I turn on the blinker and make a quicker than expected turn on the gravel road. My back end slides a little.

"Wake up crazy."

The last thing I need is to get stuck or have an accident. I slow and drive down the small gravel road. Once under control I realize that I am not cold anymore and the heater is doing its job.

THE LOST ART

"Thank God for heaters."

I pass several signs that indicate public hunting land, see open fields, and even three or four tree stands. I continue thinking about my friends that love getting out this early, sitting in a tree stand waiting for the perfect buck to walk by. You have to really love something to just sit there and wait for it to come to you. I am sure once I retire I will more than likely be doing the same thing though.

"Enjoyment comes in many different forms, might as well just have fun."

I look ahead at the Y, take the left and head down a quarter of a mile. Upon arrival, I turn the truck off and take a deep breath.

"Here we go."

I open the door and the cold air hits me like a ton of bricks.

"Holy Cow!"

I quickly walk around to the back of the truck, open the tailgate, and grab my pack. Opening the top, I look inside. I see my waders and boots. I pull them out and lay them on the tailgate. Looking over I see the river calmly rolling by. I imagine how cold the water must be. Looking on I see a ring form on the far side of the river. I continue to watch the spot and within minute's the ring forms again.

"Yes! There you are."

Seeing the distinctive ring on the surface of the water from a rising trout gets me all excited and the cold just melts away.

After seeing the trout surfacing repeatedly, I quickly grab my waders and put them on as if my life depended on it. I grab my boots and just as quickly put them on. I reached in my pack, grab my jacket, and put it on over my waders. Now I am bundled up "as snug as a bug in a rug", as my wife likes to say.

Next, I grab my rod holder and pull-out Rufus to assemble him. Rufus is a Temple Fork Outfitters, 5/6 weight, 9 ft. fly rod. Rufus may not be the most refined rod I've seen and is more ruff around the edges, much like me. He was not expensive and is the second fly rod I've had the pleasure of owning. I check Rufus' line to make sure I have the floating line and then thread the line through Rufus' eyelets. I check Rufus' leader to see if there are any wind knots and if the line is straight. Then look to see if there is enough tippet on the end. "Of course, why would there be enough?" I only want to get my feet in the river and cast a line to see if Rufus and I can battle with the multicolored fish making rings on the surface of this beautiful river."

THE LOST ART

I check my chest pack for my tippet and find the 5x tippet. This will be perfect for the trout in this river. I snip off a two-foot section and tie it onto Rufus' leader.

"Perfect." I look in my chest pack for my flies.

"Rufus, what fly do you think we should go with today?"

Rufus just sits there, leaning against my truck, ignoring me, much like my dogs did this morning while getting out of bed.

"Right, a nymph is what I was thinking too."

I take a gold bead reddish/brown nymph and decide that this would be the one. I close up the chest pack and tie the nymph onto Rufus' newly replaced tippet. I then grab an indicator, tie it on the leader about 4 foot above the nymph.

"This will help Rufus."

Rufus knows that using an indicator isn't really the preferred method but given our current situation it will work just fine. After all I did forget to bring all my dry flies.

(Quick tip; when packing for a fishing trip you need to be sure to pack everything you may or may not need. It is better to have it with you and not use it, then to get there and realize you don't have what you need.)

"I know Rufus, lesson learned."

Rufus again just looked at me as if I were crazy and just stood there in silence, probably laughing at me inside.

"Almost ready Rufus. Only thing left is the coffee."

I go back to the cab of the truck and grab my thermos and walk back to Rufus.

"It would be one long morning without this."

I put the thermos in my backpack, sling it over my shoulders, grab Rufus and head toward the river. As I walk over, I again see the trout from earlier, still making rings on the surface and I get even more excited.

I grab Rufus and prep him to cast into the river. I know we can't start casting the line directly to the rising trout, so we cast closest to our side of the river upstream. Rufus and I start false casting his line making quick movements front and back, feeding line out until there is approximately twenty feet. I then make one final false cast to get the line exactly where I want and let it go. Rufus then thrusts the line straight up the river just to the left side of the main current.

"Perfect Rufus."

THE LOST ART

I lift Rufus slowly as the line floats back to me. I strip in line to keep it straight in case the multicolored trout decides to take the meal I so carefully prepared. I can then quickly set the hook and bring the multicolored trout to me for a visit. I do this over and over working my way across the river toward the rising trout I had seen earlier.

"Next cast will be right in its path. Be ready".

Together Rufus and I made the perfect cast right in the path of the trout. Again, I lift Rufus as the line floats back to me striping in line. Then my indicator slips under the water without any big movement or splash.

"Hit it, Rufus!" I quickly thrust upward and make a short crisp strip.

"Bingo, fish on!"

The multicolored trout decided having a nymph attack him was a bad omen and took off like a bullet up the river. As the trout ran up the river I allow line to feed through my hand, Rufus' eyelets, and down toward the trout. This allowed the extra line to get extended out and the reel to buzz.

"I love it when a fish strips out line. Almost better than....."

The fish then darts in a new direction down river toward me.

THE LOST ART OF FISHING STORIES

"No! Reel! Faster, faster, faster!!!!!!! Pay attention!"

Just as abruptly as the first time the trout darted in another direction. I counter by moving Rufus toward my left shoulder. The fish seems to be getting tired now. I reel him in bringing him closer and closer.

Once he is at my feet I reach over, grab the line with my hand, put Rufus under my arm, reach down with my other hand and gently pick up the trout.

"Very nice!" A fine 14-inch multicolored trout.

I have no reason to take the fish home as a dinner guest, so I tell Rufus "We'll let him go to fight us again another day."

This time Rufus is slightly nodding up and down, I take that as he agrees and I let the trout swim out of my hand, back into his river to think heavily on the nymph that took him to see a god like creature that had his life in the palm of his hands, and his partner; a 9-ft. skinny sidekick that seems to bobble his head in agreement at everything the god like creature said.

Once I released the trout into the river, a little more educated than before, I look at Rufus' frozen eyelets and decide we would take a break to warm up.

"Rufus, let's get some coffee."

THE LOST ART

Rufus, slowly nodded, indicating he too was cold and wanted to warm up.

On the way, I remove ice from Rufus' eyelets, and he seems to perk up. I lay him down to warm himself in the sun. Taking my pack off, I lay it on the ground next to Rufus. Quickly opening the top, I grab my thermos, open it, and pour myself a cup.

"It's sure chilly out today."

Not being able to wait any longer, I took a sip of coffee.

"Mmmmmm, delicious. Nothing like a cup of coffee to warm you up. You sure you don't want any Rufus?"

Rufus sits there soaking in what little sun was showing.

"Suit yourself, Rufus."

Setting the thermos down a flood of memories take over. I think back to my father and all the advice he gave me. In fact, there are so many things in my life that without the influence of my father I would not be who and where I am today.

He would always tell me it is important to be a gentleman. He made me open the door for my mom and if I forgot would quickly say,

"Hey boy, get back here! Open the door for your mother."

He always held me to that standard. My mom, God bless her, supported my father no matter what the weather was like outside. If I forgot she would just stand there quietly waiting for me to come back and open the door. They made a great team.

Mom would say, "a wife should praise her husband in public, and criticize in private."

She lives by this and supported him this way their entire marriage. My father's chivalry taught me how I was supposed to act as a man. Seeing how my mother and father interacted together; supporting one another and showing love for one another; has set me up for success as an adult.

I have always told myself, "I want what they have."

Luckily God was watching and helped me find a great woman when I was in sixth grade. It took a while but finally in the eleventh grade she became my girlfriend. Two short years later we were married and have been going strong for seventeen years. Now that I'm a little older, I see that my father (in teaching me to be a gentlemen) and parents (showing me how to be in love) has made our marriage a success.

My friends comment on how I open the door for my wife and trying to make it to the passenger door before she gets out to

THE LOST ART

open it. They say I "go hood sliding like Bo Duke" to make it in time; although not exactly true. They also comment on how "lovey dovey" my wife and I are when we go out together.

I guess being a gentleman and showing your love is a form of a "Lost Art". This lost art, in my opinion, is not being passed on from generation to generation. Unfortunately, too many men think this type of behavior is outdated; while too many women feel they are independent and don't need a man to help them.

I look over at Rufus and say,

"Make sure I always keep this "Lost Art" and never forget it."

Rufus lays on the rock as if saying,

"Trust me, I will!"

I take one last sip of my coffee.

"I'm good to go now Rufus. You ready?"

Rufus says nothing and continues napping on the rocks. I return the silver cap on the thermos, put the thermos in my pack, and throw the pack on. I pick Rufus up.

"Ready or not we are moving on."

As I pick him up, he starts nodding up and down agreeing in his usual way. We start our journey up the bank looking for the best spot to enter the river and continue our fishing adventure.

I see a log in quick moving water up ahead.

"Let's start here and work our way up."

I unhook the nymph from his eyelet and let the line fall loose. I walk to the river's edge, raise Rufus, and let the line fly thru the air. I false cast pulling line off the spool to have enough line to make a good cast. I make a final false cast and let Rufus toss the line by the fast water closest to the edge of the river. I work my way back and forth along the river, one side to the other, trying to get my nymph in a seam that a trout would be sitting.

After working across the river several times, the indicator is pulled under the water. I quickly lift Rufus to set the hook. Rufus bends over and looks directly at the fish. We feel the fish pull to the right across the river. I walk upriver trying not to lose the tension on the fish. I add pressure to move the fish and all of a sudden, the fish spits out the hook and swims away.

Rufus bobs his head as if saying, "Not so much pressure. Relax! Take your time."

"I know, I know. Give me a break!"

We move back and cast again. As we continue the cast, drift, cast again motions of river fishing I think back to the stories my father told of his Marine Corps experience. In one boot camp story, he was instructed to report to his drill instructor (DI) inside the duty hut. Standing next to the door, he took a step forward, pivoted left to enter the door and saw his DI standing in his way. Hesitating, the DI pushed him out the door causing him to fall on the floor.

"Try again Private Cox!"

Dad got up, stood next to the door, stepped forward, pivoting into the doorway. Again, the DI standing there tossed him out. Now in a much louder and gruff voice, "

"No! Try again Private Cox."

My father not one to take anything for too long told himself "I'm not going to let this happen again", and for the third time he stepped forward, pivoted into the doorway, lowered his shoulder, and rammed directly into his DI. Pushing the DI back almost knocking him on the floor, saying,

"Sir, Private Cox reporting as ordered."

"Why didn't you do that the first time. Nothing stands in the way of a Marine. If you don't make the mark the first time, then try again until you make it."

Just like dad, I took the DIs advice prepping to catch the fish.

My father, yet again, passed another "Lost Art" to me.

"If at first you don't succeed, then try, try again."

Taking my father's advice, Rufus and I tried again and were successful in hooking and landing one more beautiful rainbow trout. Four hours on the river in the freezing cold was a good enough trip for today. I look over at Rufus and once again he is frozen over with ice looking beat down with cold.

"Ok Rufus, time to head to the barn. I still have to go visit family today."

Rufus nods slowly in agreement as if saying, "It's about time boss."

As we walk back to the truck, I admire the river. I lived only ten miles from this fishing Mecca and never tapped in. I had a different idea of what my priorities were then. I spent hours honing my skills as a musician knowing one day, I would make a living utilizing this craft. As a Marine musician, I have performed for President's, Senator's, General's, and foreign dignitaries all over the world. Being a Marine musician has been the second-best decision I have done in my adult life. The first decision: marrying my wife.

We make it back to the truck and I pack everything up. I pull Rufus apart saying.

"Don't worry Rufus, we will get together tomorrow to continue our adventures."

As I pull him apart, he seems to be happy to get in his warm cozy case to rest up for the next day's journey. I put my pack on the tailgate in order to get my thermos. I pour one last cup of coffee and continue to pack. I think to myself, if it wasn't for my father, I wouldn't even be a fly fisherman. I get in the truck and start the fifteen-minute ride back to my father-in-law's house.

I only remember fishing with dad about five times. Dad never really taught me anything about fishing itself and in fact I don't think we were successful, but the one thing I remember is he had a fly rod. I always thought it was a majestic way of fishing, seeing his line making looping designs in the air. I am sure he didn't realize his fly fishing would impact me years later.

I was 30 years old before I decided to even think about picking up a fly rod. As I watched a fly-fishing program I said, "If I were going to start fishing this is exactly the type of fishing I would do." My father, not even around anymore, has once again influenced my decision and passed on to me a desire to learn another "Lost Art".

It was another six months before I actually went to a fly-fishing store to purchase a fly rod in Chicago of all places, but since then I have spent many hours practicing this art and learning as much as I could about this great sport. Unfortunately, dad wasn't around to share this art, but he did inspire me to learn and keep a tradition of another "Lost Art".

"Thanks for the great fishing dad. Love ya."

About this time, I drive up to my father-in-law's house and walk inside. Both my wife and father-in-law are sitting in the living room and greet me with a smile and a question.

"Get anything?"

They both know that there are many times I go fishing and never even get a bite. I pause and think about the two-beautiful fish I caught, but more importantly the reflection of my life and how much my family and friends mean to me. Yes, it was a very productive fishing trip indeed. I just smile back.

"I caught about six. The smallest was about 14 inches and the largest was about twenty inches."

Got to love fish stories!

Story 2:
Surf Fishing

Surf Fishing

As I open the garage door, Olga is staring at me. Olga, a 750cc, 2-wheel drive, green Ural motorcycle with sidecar, was born in Russia and shipped to the United States. This morning we are going to the San Diego beach to do my favorite past time, Fly Fishing.

"Good morning, Olga."

Still tired, she said nothing. I walked to my fishing gear, picked up my chest pack, then looked on the garage wall where I had my fly rods hanging.

"Sorry Rufus, not this time. You're not stout enough for the surf."

I looked at the other fly rods hanging on the wall.

"Shorty, it's you and me today."

Shorty, a stout 7' 11", Sage, Largemouth Bass rod. Shorter and stouter than my other rods, he can make quicker deliveries with larger flies and is better suited for the surf.

I pulled Shorty off the wall and out of his case just far enough to look at the reel. The black line on the reel indicated the sinking line was on and ready to go.

I then reached over and grabbed my stripping basket that is worn on the hip. Unlike conventional fishing, fly fishing does not utilize the reel to pull in the line after casting. Instead, the fisherman pulls the line in by hand and places the line in the stripping basket.

Walking my gear to Olga, I place it in the sidecar. Olga is very well designed for fishing trips. There is plenty of space to put all my fishing gear and enough space to pack several day's worth of camping gear.

In fact, my wife and I have been on many weekend trips riding Olga. There is enough space in the sidecar for my wife to sit comfortably and we put our bags in the sidecar trunk or strap it down on the top. Yes, I said trunk. Olga gets lots of attention no matter where we go. People stop to ask all kinds of questions. Ural riders call this UDF (Ural Delay Factor).

UDF has made me late for many fishing adventures and even late for work. One time we had stopped at a gas station for gas and to take a break. When we returned, there were seven or eight people standing around Olga talking about her. Of course, Olga just sat there and didn't answer any questions. I walked up and almost in unison the spectators said,

"This yours?"

"Yes sir."

"Awesome bike. We were just talking about it."

I decided I would do my favorite thing when there is someone asking questions about Olga.

"I have ten dollars for anyone that can guess the year she was made."

They quickly started guessing.

"1955. 1963. 1949. 1935. 1970."

Pretty much everything except the correct year. After several minutes of guessing I said,

"Not even close. She was made in 2010."

After hearing this they really started to inspect her and got even closer to see. I explained that the company still makes their bikes with the same basic design as they did when the company started around 1940. They have added newer features, but the look of the bike is still basically the same, which is why I still have the same $10 in my pocket.

After loading Olga with all my fishing gear, I opened the garage door and pulled her out into the crisp California air.

"Time to wake up and go for a ride Olga."

I reached over, turned the key to the on position, put her into neutral, and kick started her. It took me 4 times for her to turn over. I could have used the electric starter, but I enjoy doing things the way they did "back in the day."

"Olga, why do I act older than I am?"

She just continued to purr not paying attention to my crazy talk. I click the button and close the garage.

Olga smoothed out and I throw my leg over her and sat down. After putting her in gear I ease out the clutch and give her some gas. She jumps out of the driveway and is eager to get going.

"Alright Olga, just let me check traffic. You know how traffic is here in Southern California."

She revved her engine saying. "Yes! Absolutely crazy."

We took off toward the beach. While driving I notice that everyone out this morning is very fast paced and not at all in touch with "the good old days". I look at all the fancy cars parked along the road and realize that there are very few individuals that even know how to change the oil in their cars anymore.

I laugh and look over to see a group of people on a run. Every person had earphones in and were each listening to their own music. I can't understand that if you are running with someone

SURF FISHING

why you would have music playing and not talking with your running partner. Seems a little rude to me. I guess that is just me still living in the past.

Again, I laugh and say, "Olga, be sure to slap me if I start acting that way."

We turn the corner to the parking lot and there are several parking spaces still available. Sometimes there are none due to the surfers. They are just as fanatical about surfing as fishermen are about fishing. I park in the closest parking spot. After turning Olga off I walk around to the sidecar and pull my shoes off to put my boots on. I use boots in the surf, so I don't get stung by a stingray while fishing.

I take out my chest pack and put it on. I attach the stripping basket and pull Shorty out of the case. While putting Shorty together a man walked by holding his surfboard.

"Good morning."

As usual the individual just looks at me and keeps on walking. This is one of the things I can't stand about Southern California. Most individuals that are from this area do not act very friendly. If you try to talk to them, they ignore you. I guess it has to do with the fact I am not from their area.

I think to myself, if I would have ignored someone when they said something to me growing up, my father would have had some words with me. In my opinion the word rude comes up again.

"Shorty, I guess that is the difference between small town USA and big city USA."

By this time, Shorty was completely put together and was shaking his head up and down in agreeance.

"Yes sir, yes sir. That's the difference boss. You betchya."

I walk down the boardwalk taking in the sights. There are several motivators running, others are waiting patiently for the sunrise, and others are heading out to ride the waves in the rising sunlight.

I find my normal starting point and walk out in the sand.

"Well Shorty, how does the normal starting point sound to you?"

Shorty nods his head as we walk toward the water,

"Yes sir, let's get started."

As we reach the water, I wade into the surf waist deep and start casting. The line whips through the air until I feel we have enough line. I make one last heave and throw the line as far as possible. As the line sinks I back slowly toward the beach keeping the slack out of the line. After allowing the line to sink I start stripping the line back letting it coil in the stripping basket.

The fish along the beach love shrimp and crab patterns. This time I have a pink shrimp pattern. I have a short leader of about 5 feet and only 2 feet of tippet on the leader.

I strip in line and recast as I walk south along the beach. As we continue fishing, I look at the sun just rising over the ocean and feel it's warmth starting to do its job. I am amazed at how beautiful the San Diego sunrise is. It is truly a site that everyone should see.

The only other sunrise that I have seen that compares would be a desert sunrise. It is so big and beautiful you have to be in awe that anyone could deny there is a God to create it. In fact, the best sunrise I have ever seen was while I was deployed to Iraq. I was on one of the guard towers overlooking the Euphrates River when the sun was rising. It was the biggest sunrise I had ever seen.

It always amazed me that I was in the land of bible times. The story I remember most that took place in Iraq was the story of Daniel and the lion's den. Unfortunately, I didn't get to see the site firsthand but there were several of my Marines that did. If there was ever a time to be jealous, that was it.

Shorty and I continue throwing the pink shrimp pattern and get ready for the sign that there is a fish on the end of the line. I look over and see a rip tide. This is the perfect spot. The fish stay on the outside of the rip tide, much like trout in a river, waiting for unsuspecting prey. The fish will dart in quickly, grab the prey, and dart back out enjoying his reward for being patient.

We make our way down casting closer then I feel a tug on the line. I lift Shorty quickly to set the hook.

"Fish On."

As I stripped the line in, placing it in the stripping basket, Shorty is bent over bowing toward the fish. I can feel the fish trying to dart in and out of the waves and I also feel the waves pulling back toward open water making the fight even better.

We continue our dance and I notice several individuals watching on the beach. Once I have the fish close enough, I reach down and pick him up. A great looking Surf Perch.

The individuals watching came over.

"We've never seen anyone catch anything on the beach. It kind of scares us a little."

I smile and say in a confident voice,

SURF FISHING

"If you haven't been eaten yet, the chances are slim to none."

After catching a surf perch, I was feeling pretty good. I wanted to quickly get back to fishing, so I checked the line and sent the pink shrimp pattern back into the surf.

I continued fishing up the shore waiting again for the tell-tell sign of a fish taking my fly. After fighting my way up, the shore in the surf for 10 minutes I decided to change my fly and see if I could get another fish.

"Shorty let's put on a crab pattern and see what happens."

I tied on a small crab pattern and whipped the line back into the surf. As I was stripping the line in, I felt a tug on the line. I raised the rod to set the hook.

The fish didn't take off. Instead, it felt like I was hung up on something. I lowered the rod and started attempting to pull it in different direction to get the hook free from the obstruction. On the third pull, the line got really tight, and the reel started buzzing.

"Hold on Shorty."

The line quickly continued running out as the fish easily swam through the surf. It was as if the surf didn't bother the fish at all. I continued to work the fish toward shore, but the fish had other plans. It darted up shore and I clumsily made my way through the waves trying to keep up.

I was now in the backing on the reel, didn't have much line left, and knew I had better do something quick. I lifted the rod to the right to change the direction of the fish. There was a strong pull from the fish but eventually he did turn and make a run back down the beach in the opposite direction. I was able to reel in some line and gain the upper hand. Not much later the fish got his second wind and took off like a bat out of hell.

I made my way back down the shore knowing that I would lose the line I gained in a matter of seconds.

"Dang, we need to work a little harder. This fish is just man handling us."

I put a little more force on Shorty. I thought he may break under the pressure but decided to just go for it anyway. As we applied more force the fish started slowly coming toward shore.

It was twenty minutes before the fish was close enough to shore to see. I had never hooked anything this powerful in the surf before and was excited to get it on shore.

When the fish was close enough, I backed up letting the waves bring the fish on the beach where I could get to it easily. I walked over to it, and I didn't recognize the fish.

"I don't know what we have Shorty. Stingray or shark?"

As I was checking to make sure there was no stinger on the fish, a man walked up.

"I watched that whole fight. I am impressed. I didn't know you could fly fish on the beach or even get something this big."

"I am a little surprised myself, sir. This is the biggest fish I have gotten on the beach yet."

I reached down, picked up the ten-pound guitarfish (Looked it up when I got home) , and walked it back into the surf releasing it.

Looking back at my spectator I said, "too bad I don't have a camera today."

With my confidence in the clouds, I got my fly line back in the water. It didn't take long before I again had another large fish trying to manhandle me and Shorty. It felt much like the guitarfish that gave us such a fight before.

Adrenaline surging, I utilized the lesson learned from the guitarfish in fighting this new monster of the deep. It didn't take long for the fish to run into my backing. It was almost as if the reel was smoking due to how fast it was moving. I put my left hand against the reel to add drag and help slow the fish down.

The fish felt this, turned, and darted toward us. I started reeling the line in so not to lose tension in the line. The fish kept running toward us. At this moment, I remembered a movie.

There they were, standing on the beach just having a great time, swimming, boating, and tubing. No problems at all. Not even a care in the world.

The camera flashes to a young women swimming. There is a shot of a fin on top of the water. Then, the young woman is pulled under the water down to the depths becoming a sweet appetizer for the giant shark that ends up going around eating just about everyone possible.

"Shorty, I hope to God this isn't a shark! If it is, you are on your own."

Shorty just ignored me and kept fighting the fish as best he could. About thirty feet from us the fish turned up the shoreline and took another run. We countered and tried to bring the fish back toward us.

It took three more runs and we finally had the fish on shore. The fish was a stingray. Not just a stingray, but an extremely upset stingray. So upset that it was trying to sting anything even close to it.

As I walk up to it, I think, "How in the world am I going to get this fish back in the water"? I had no gloves or gear to be able to pick up a stingray. A young lady walked up and was watching me.

"You need to get the stingray back in the water. I can't even believe you are fishing here. You shouldn't be allowed."

Great! A hippie woman who thinks no one should ever harm anything. This should be fun.

"Don't worry lady. I'll get it back in the water."

I sat there thinking, probably looking dumbfounded, and decided to use Shorty to push the fish back in the water. I used Shorty to hold down the stinger as I took out the fly. I then turned Shorty around and used the butt end to push the stingray. The stingray would only move when the waves come up and I give a good hard shove.

I did this three times and then on the fourth time Shorty caved under the pressure.

"SNAP!"

I WENT RED! I got so upset that I am sure I embarrassed the young lady, who looked all of eighteen, standing next to me by my very colorful language. After losing my cool for about thirty seconds I realized what I was doing, looked over at the lady (by this time there were four other people standing around).

"I'm sorry. Really, I'm sorry."

I finished pushing the stingray in the surf, turned around, and headed toward the parking lot as quickly as I could.

"Shorty, I just went from hero to zero! Time to tuck tail and run."

Story 3: Like a Pro

50

Like a Pro

As I put my Kayak in the bed of my truck I knew it was going to be a great day fishing. As I lifted the Kayak I thought, "Where do I want to go fishing?"

In the San Diego area, I had lots of great fishing destinations to utilize my kayak. There are plenty of lakes with Bass, Catfish, Bluegill, and even Trout. Then there are the different Bays. San Diego Bay and Mission Bay. There is a plethora of fish in both bays. Spotted and Sand Bass, Bonefish, Halibut, Sharks, Corvina, Croaker, Barracuda, and Bonita to name a few.

I strapped down the kayak and turned to get my faithful fly rod, Slim. Slim, a 9ft 8 weight Temple Fork Outfitter fly rod was the 1st fly rod I ever owned. I actually purchased him when my wife brought me along with her to a foster care/adoption conference she attended in Chicago. While she was at the conference I was left alone to my own devices and was a little bored out of my mind.

My wife, being the great wife that she is, knew I had been talking about fly fishing for a while and looked up a fly-fishing store there in Chicago and told me to go check it out. Of course, like any good husband I said, "Yes Ma'am" and left the hotel first chance I got.

My wife is great at doing things for others. She has an ability to listen to people and pick out great gifts that match each person perfectly. Me, being the typical male, doesn't pay attention to anything and can't ever match her when it is time to get her a gift. Maybe someday I will actually be able to get her the perfect gift.

After reaching the fly-fishing store I spent about three hours there asking question after question about fly fishing and eventually purchased Slim. It was the start of a great friendship. Slim has been with me through many fishing trips and once again was going to join me today.

As I was placing Slim in my truck I asked, "Slim, where do you want to go fishing today?"

Slim just nodded excitedly saying, "Wherever you want boss. Yep, wherever you want!"

"Well, I think it would be best to fish Mission Bay. The tides seem to be just right, and I think the bay bass are getting more active."

Slim again nodded in enthusiastically, "You bet boss, yes sir! Mission Bay it is!"

I got in the truck and headed down the road toward Mission Bay. Since the bay is only four miles from the house it doesn't take long at all to get there to start my favorite past time.

As I pull up to the boat launch there is a large bay boat unloading and I think how awesome it would be to have a larger boat. Oh well, maybe someday I will be able to afford one.

I park close to the boat launch in order to have a shorter distance to travel. I unload the kayak from the back and strap the kayak wheels to the bottom in order to move it easier. I then load the kayak with my day pack. I put my fishing gear inside the pack along with some coffee in my favorite thermos and some snacks just in case I get a little hungry. I do have a tendency to stay on the water longer if I don't get a bite or catch a fish. I hate to get skunked.

After loading the kayak, I grab Slim, "Here we go Slim. It's a beautiful day to catch some fish."

I grab the kayak and pull it down to the boat launch. By the time I get there the larger boat that was launching had already pulled off and was heading out on the water. Once by the water I pulled the wheels off and put them inside the kayak. I then opened up the pontoons on the back to stabilize the kayak.

My kayak is a Freedom Hawk Kayak and has two pontoons that will come out by pulling levers on each side. This allows the individual in the kayak to have a stable platform to do stand-up fishing. Fly casting while sitting down is a little difficult and way easier from the standing position. This also allows a better platform to do sight fishing. The pontoons are then pulled in while paddling to get from place to place faster.

Once I get the kayak in the water and I get loaded, I then have a seat, pull the pontoons in, and start paddling toward the bridge.

My favorite way of fishing this area is to drift in the kayak on an incoming tide with my line trolling behind the kayak. I use a sinking line in order to get down in the water column where the sand and spotted bass like to stay. The best fly that I have found to use is a chartreuse, bright green, clouser. This is a baitfish pattern and works wonders with fish in the bays. The other fly that works well is a smaller clouser pattern that looks much like a shrimp pattern in the water.

As I paddle toward the bridge to start drift fishing, I see many boats out on the water. There are large boats on their way to the open ocean, smaller bay boats, jet skis, and other individuals in Kayaks just enjoying the bay. During the summer, there are always many people out in the bays enjoying the wonderful San Diego sun. I am just one of many. There aren't that many people actually fishing but that doesn't stop me at all, I know there are fish that need to be caught.

As I pull under the bridge, I let out the pontoons, stand up, and grab Slim.

"Alright Slim, let's get started."

I take Slim and together we start casting line out in order to hopefully catch one of the large bay bass swimming under my kayak.

Swoosh, Swoosh, Swoosh! As Slim and I cast line out, I think how close the line and fly passes by my head. I start to laugh and remember when I first started fly fishing. I was out on this very bay, Mission Bay, and had a large clouser pattern on the end of the line. I had not become very proficient with casting and was practicing getting the line out further and further.

I had not yet realized you have to be cautious and know which way the wind is blowing because the wind can blow the line and fly wherever it wants. There are different techniques in order to still cast in the wind, but I had not yet learned them.

There I was thinking I was doing pretty good casting, getting the line out to at least thirty feet or so. Just like today I heard the Swoosh, Swoosh, Swoosh of the line passing close by my head. I wound up and sent the fly by my head to the front. I watched the fly go out to the end of the line and pulled back to do one last cast.

Still watching the fly at the end of the line, I watched it as it traveled closer and closer to me. In fact, everything went into slow motion. The fly inched its way toward my face. I thought to myself, "Crap, get out of the way!" I for some reason just couldn't move fast enough.

Still watching the fly, it inched even closer. "It's going to put my eye out!" Just like in the movie The Christmas Story and the kid was told "you'll shoot your eye out", here I am with my own version of a b-b-gun (fly rod, line, and fly) and just like the young kid I was going to "shoot my eye out".

The fly, ever so slow, kept coming toward my head. I could see the fly inching its way getting larger and larger than all of a sudden "Thump". I shout out in pain and immediately reach up and grab my face.

First things first; Did I shoot out my eye? I slowly open my eyes and feel with my hands to make sure the fly didn't hook my eye. Thankfully, both eyes were intact, and I could see just fine. I looked down and saw the fly on the bottom of the Kayak and realized it didn't actually hook me anywhere.

I reached up and felt a knot on my forehead just starting to form. How lucky can someone get?

At this time, the man factors kick in. I quickly look around to see who saw me just make a fool of myself. "Thank God. Slim that could have been embarrassing."

No one was there with a camera to film my fishing bloopers like all my favorite fishing hero's, Bill Dance and the Great American Fisherman Roland Martin.

LIKE A PRO

With my line trolling behind me, my kayak floating with the incoming tide, and me diligently stripping in line to make my clouser look like an injured bait fish, I suddenly realize that I am the only fisherman on the water right now. I take a glance around and see a large boat pulling out of the nearby docs heading out to possibly fish for larger game.

Up the bay I see a team of rowers in a professional racing rowboat. Not far behind them is another rowboat that seems to be in a race against one another. I can see how rowing can be an excellent form of exercise. Maybe I might try it some time.

I get to the end of the fishing line and recast the clouser to get it back into action. I hear the distinct Swoosh sound as the fly and line go by my head. Slim is working great today. Easily sending the clouser at least fifty to sixty feet before letting the fly and line settle into the water.

I let the line settle to a count of ten in order to get it down to the water column best suited for bay bass. I then start my ritual of stripping in line with a short, short, long stripping pattern. This has landed me a many fish and is a great pattern to use.

I continue drifting further away from the bridge and still no bites. I end up casting out and stripping the line in a total of 4 times and know I need to re-paddle up to the bridge and start the drift again. I use the reel to bring the line in this time and leave about twenty feet still dragging behind the kayak. I place the rod in the rod holder at the rear of the kayak, sit down, pull in the pontoons, and start paddling back to the bridge.

As I paddle back there are a couple of young boys riding jet skis. Where I am, it is a no wake zone, so there are no large waves that I get from boats but with these young boys not knowing the rules they decide they want to go by me at mock two. They come from my back-right side and fly by me like I am standing still, and they are a fighter jet on a mission to drop a bomb on the enemy.

After they pass, I know that I am in for a ride. I look over my shoulder and see the large waves coming my way. When they reach me, I tell slim, "Hold on bud. It's going to be a rough ride."

Just as I thought, the kayak started bucking like we were riding rapids down a river in Colorado. I thought for sure it was going to throw me and I was going to swim with the fish in the ocean but then just as quick as the waves came up, they died out.

I looked up to see where the jet skis were, and they were long gone.

"I really hope they don't come by like that again. Especially if I'm standing. That won't be a good ride."

LIKE A PRO

I look over my shoulder to see if Slim is still with me and he is bent over trying to look down at the water. I quickly shoot out the pontoons so I can stand. This is a sign that there is a fish that has finally took my clouser for breakfast.

I stand up and grab Slim. As I lift Slim up, I feel the fish on the end of the line fighting for his breakfast.

"Here we go Slim."

I start reeling line in and it feels like I'm reeling in dead weight. As I continue to reel in line there is no more fighting back. Just heavy slow reeling. As it begins to surface, I see that it is not a fish at all but a large patch of seaweeds.

"Oh well Slim. I guess it was good practice."

After paddling back up to the bridge, I put the pontoons out and between Slim and my efforts we again cast the fly about fifty feet out. I let the line sink again. This time on number six in my count to ten I feel a tug on my line.

"Set it Slim." Slim and I set the hook and get ready for a good fight.

The fish not wanting to be pulled up toward the surface turned and swam toward the bottom of the bay. Slim bent over further and looked as if there were a 100-pound fish on the line. The reel started buzzing and I knew we definitely didn't have seaweed on the line this time.

We countered the fish and pulled him to the right. He reluctantly went to the right. Then instead of pulling back to the bottom he kept trying to out swim my counter. I quickly countered the other way pulling him to the left. This time he was not having it and kept pulling to the right. It was a struggle between man and fish. Lucky for me I had Slim on my side and between the two of us we continued our mission of bringing the giant bay bass to the surface.

Seeing that the leader was coming out of the water now I knew the fish wasn't far behind. I continue reeling in line and then see the bass. It is a spotted bay bass. He was a good 3-pound fish and was absolutely wore out from the fight.

I reached down and grabbed the fish and brought it in the boat with Slim and I. "Now we're talking Slim. I think things are looking up."

I took a picture or two and released the bass back into the bay to fight again at a later date. I quickly grabbed Slim and started casting to get back in the fight. That all familiar "Swoosh" again came whizzing by reminding me to be ever aware of the direction of the wind in order to not but heads with the fly on the end of the line.

I let the line sink and started stripping line in. Short, short, long. Short, short, long. We cast out again and continue the ritual. We again feel the thrilling tug on the end of the line.

"Slim, they are all awake now."

We had a good 5-minute fight and caught another bass. This time it was a sand bass. The difference is the sand bass has more of a striped coloring and the spotted bay bass is as the fish is named, spots all over it.

We continue our drift recasting and catching fish after fish. I get to the end of the drift and prepare for another paddle back up to the bridge. I place slim in his rod holder, pull in the pontoons and paddle toward the bridge.

On the way to the bridge, I see a boat that seems to be watching and even taking photos and videos of me. I paddle all the way back to the bridge and prep for the next drift. As I stand up and start casting again, I notice the boat driving over to me. I let the line drift behind the boat and check out what the boat was doing.

A man on the boat looked at me and asked if he could come over next to my kayak.

"Sure, no problem."

The boat come over and I grabbed the side. The man asked if I do much fishing here and said they were with the weather channel. They were doing a show about the lifeguards that worked the Bay. He asked if he could film me fishing and put me on the show.

By this time, I am feeling really good about myself and tell them I would be happy to. The boat gets my info and lets me know when the show will air then pulls back to film me fishing.

I grab Slim and say, "Slim, we are officially going to be TV stars."

Slim nods up and down saying, "Yes sir boss. About time boss."

With my new-found camera crew, I could just hear the theme song playing in my head, "He's the great American Fisherman, He'll fish anywhere, anywhere there's water, Lord knows that he'll be there!"

I picked up Slim and we started our first on camera experience. Together we made the most beautiful cast I have ever made. The Swoosh came close to my head, and I just knew that from the camera angle it would be a great shot. I acted as professional as I could and tried to make every movement very deliberate. I pulled in the line with my patented short, short, long pattern. I just knew that any moment the fish would take my fly and make me look like the professional I thought I was.

LIKE A PRO

I continued to pull in the line. "Nothing". That's OK. You can't get a fish every cast. Slim and I wound up again and made another incredible cast. Swoosh, back and forth, and then we let it fly. At least sixty-five feet. The longest cast I have made today.

"Slim, they will for sure use that footage. That was awesome!"

Slim nodded, "Yes sir, boss. For sure!"

I continued the drift and with each cast the camera crew followed, watching and waiting for that perfect moment when I land a fish. We drifted down for at least 15 more minutes to my normal turning point. I turned around and put Slim in the rod holder.

"We'll make one more pass. I'm sure we will get a fish."

I started paddling back toward the bridge and glanced over to make sure the camera crew was following me, only to see them speeding off down the bay.

"I can't believe it Slim; this was our chance to be famous and we didn't get one stinking fish."

By this time, I was now a little frustrated. I really wanted to look good on my video debut. When I got back to the bridge Slim, and I made a cast but not nearly as good as we had been doing. I continued my short, short, long pattern and knew I would get a bite. Then all of a sudden, I got snagged on something. I pulled but couldn't get it undone. I had to paddle back up to lessen the tension then finally it came loose.

"That was close Slim. Almost lost my good fly. Maybe we had better call it quits."

I decided to leave the fly line out behind me to troll while heading back to the boat launch. As I was paddling, I thought to myself how awesome it was to have someone film me. I was feeling pretty good about myself and knew that Slim enjoyed it. I couldn't wait to get home to tell my wife and friends about the experience.

All of a sudden, I heard a thump from behind me. I turned around just in time to hear a splash. When I finally realized, what had happened, I panicked. There was Slim being pulled right out of the rod holder. I couldn't believe it. I quickly tried to turn the kayak to get back to slim. He was just on the surface of the water barely floating. The kayak was taking forever to turn. It seemed like it was an ocean liner. It felt like hours.

I finally got it turned and headed toward Slim. Slim now was just barely had his head at the surfaced of the water. As I approached, I tried to grab him to pull him to safety. I reached for him, but he fell deeper in the water. I knew I would pass him again and there was no way he would last for another pass so I did what any professional fisherman would do. I DOVE IN AFTER HIM.

As I dove, I reached for him and just felt him with my fingertips. He continued to sink. I went under the water to try and find him but no such luck. He was now swimming at the bottom of the bay.

I surfaced from the water and my blood was boiling. It felt like the water around me was a good ten to fifteen degrees warmer now due to my temperature rising. As I surfaced, I screamed words that for sure professional fisherman do not use on camera. I quickly got in my kayak and paddled to shore as a beaten and battered fighter at the end of the last round just embarrassed by his defeat leaving the arena.

Thank God the camera crew didn't see this debacle. It could have rivaled Bill Dance with his fishing bloopers. The paddle back to shore was the longest paddle I had ever done, and I just knew that my wife and friends would never let me live this one down.

RIP Slim. Meet Slim Jr.

Story 4:
Big Man Upstairs

My father, Leonard Eugene Cox, fishing.

Big Man Upstairs

With my line trolling behind the boat and Shorty and I drifting in the wind, I look around and enjoy the beautiful view. The lake always looks incredible this time of year. It didn't take long for Shorty to be repaired, thanks to the Sage Fly Rod warranty. He was ready to get back to what he was meant to do.

The boat drifted on the small ripples due to the soft blowing wind. The sun was shining through the clouds just enough to keep everything nice and bright but not too much to make the temperature rise. I lean back, still holding onto Shorty, and lay my head on my day pack. I figure I could take a little break and relax for a while. I close my eyes to just rest them for a couple of minutes.

I can feel Shorty still being ever cautious and attentive to the line trailing behind the boat.

"Shorty, just let me know when we get a bite."

I feel him moving and I can imagine him shaking his head up and down in his agreement. The sun and wind make it perfect conditions for a quick cat nap, and I quickly doze off into a small slumber.

I am startled awake by a deep booming voice saying, "Get up son, set the hook! You're going to lose him!"

I quickly scramble to my feet rocking the boat almost causing Shorty and I to fall overboard. I raise Shorty in the air to set the hook and immediately feel the distinct tug of a fish on the other end of the line.

"Here we go Shorty, make it count." Shorty and I fight with the fish and quickly pull him on the boat. A good fourteen-inch Rainbow trout with the most beautiful coloring is now in my hands. I then realize that the voice I had heard was not Shorty at all but a different voice. One I had heard many times throughout my life.

I quickly spin around, almost throwing the fish overboard, to see who was on the boat with me. As I finished turning, I saw a man wearing all white fishing clothes. The man looked identical to my father, and I know it couldn't be, he had passed on and went to heaven seven years back.

I stood there in awe and couldn't bring myself to speak. After several minutes dad just said simply, "I'm only here for a short while son. I know we never really got any opportunities to fish together while you were growing up, but I asked God if I could get a little fishing time with my son. So here I am." He then winked at me with a crooked smile and said, "You may want to let the trout go before he ends up in heaven with me."

I then snapped back into reality and said, "Yes sir." I leaned over and let the rainbow trout swim off. I grabbed Shorty and looked back at dad. "Well dad, if there isn't much time let's get to it."

He smiled and started casting his bright white fly rod. We fished for a good hour each catching beautiful trout after trout. It was the best fishing I had ever done in my life, and I got to share it with my hero.

I said to my dad, "I wish we could have done this the whole time you were alive."

Dad looked over at me and said, "Yes it would have been fun but remember you wouldn't be where you are today if things were different. You have a wonderful wife and child in your house now. You just remember as a father to teach your children the important things in life just like I have taught you. If you do this, then your children will love you as much as you have loved me. I don't have much time left and I want to tell you, there is a large fish pulling on your line.

"What?"

"There is a large fish pulling on your line."

"Huh?"

"A large fish pulling on your line."

All of a sudden, I felt the line go ripping away from Shorty. It startled me so much I jumped up from my slumber and set the hook. As I was fighting the fish, I looked over to see if dad was watching but realized he was not on the boat with me at all.

"I get it dad, what you taught me is always with me. I love you very much."

-In loving memory of Leonard Eugene Cox. Father, Mentor, and Hero. -

If your father's still around take him fishing.

Happy Father Day!

Story 5:
Secret Honey Hole

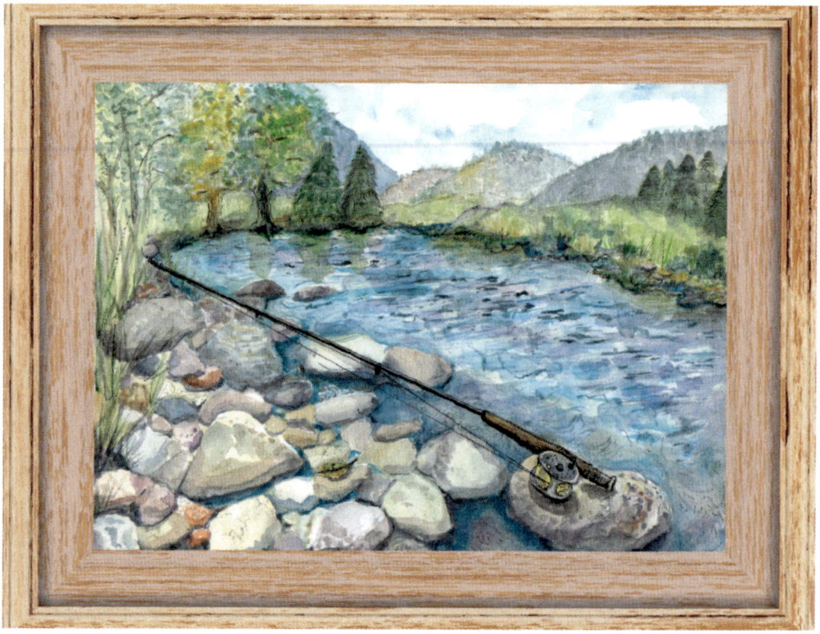

Secret Honey Hole

Sitting on the couch at my mother-in-law's house in Roland, my nephew, Aubrey, looked over and said, "We could go fishing at my secret spot where I caught all those bass I told you about."

Of course, this got me interested immediately. "Sure, sounds good to me."

He said, "Let me call my grandpa and see if he knows the code and if he will take us."

"Perfect."

Aubrey walked outside to check with his grandpa. All I could think to myself was visions of all the big bass we would be catching. From everything he has told me every cast they are catching monster bass. This means I could practice my top water skills and practice the strip set instead of the trout set. This should make for some good fishing.

I was awakened out of my daydreams by the sound of conversations about politics and current events. This always starts some interesting chats and I really try to keep my opinions to myself as best as I can, but every now and then my temper gets the best of me, and I start running off at the mouth. I guess it makes the talks interesting and I have come to realize that everyone knows what sets me off and will push my buttons just to get a rise out of me.

I always think back to some advice my dad gave me growing up. "Son, when someone is laughing at you or giving you a hard time, just smile and laugh along with them. They will eventually get tired of it because you will not have the reaction they are looking for and move on to something different."

In other words, "Turn the other cheek."

All I can say is, it's easier said than done, although, I have gotten much better at it over the years.

We continue to discuss politics and the affects it is having on the country then Aubrey walks over and says, "What about tomorrow morning? Can you go then?"

Without thinking twice, I said, "Yes." I didn't even bother to check with the wife because I am sure she will understand. After all it is *the* "Secret Honey Hole."

I again start thinking about the fishing trip and what I need to get ready. I start a list in my head of gear I need to take.

1-Slim Jr. (8 weight fly rod)
2-Rufus (4-5 weight fly rod)
3-extra reels w/ different lines (floating, intermediate, sinking)
4-Leaders

5-flies (freshwater trout and bass flies)
6-chest pack for small gear
7-backpack for all other gear
8-water

I was again awakened from my daydreams. My wife was saying, "Hold Madison so we can all go out and get pictures before everyone takes off."

I said, "Okay Sweetie, no problem." Thinking anything I do to help my wife will ease the decision of fishing at the Secret Honey Hole in the morning. I decide I would tell my wife on the way to my father-in-law's house for the night that way if she does get a little upset, it won't ruin the evening's festivities.

On the way to my father-in-law's house, I broke the news about my fishing trip to my wife and of course she was supportive and said that would be fine if I met her for lunch and went with her the rest of the day. I quickly jumped on it and said yes.

The next morning my alarm went off at 0530. I had to be at my nephew, Aubrey's house by 0700. I guess I don't have to wake up this early but the excitement of fishing the Secret Honey Hole got me extremely motivated.

I got up and showered, shaved, and got all my gear together. I grabbed a cup of coffee and headed out the door with all my fishing gear in tow.

Driving to pick up Aubrey all I could think about was the giant bass waiting for me. I imagined myself as a famous fishing TV star with my own show. I could just see me fishing from shore and catching bass after bass with enough good footage that I would easily have a highlights reel for my imaginary TV show.

I looked over at Rufus and Slim Jr. saying, "Someday we will have our own fishing series and we will all be famous."

Both Rufus and Slim Jr. just shook their heads at me as if saying, "Your crazy boss, straight crazy."

Realizing I was running out of coffee and thinking I had better get a quick bite to eat I stopped by a gas station. I got myself a cup of coffee and a sausage biscuit. Then again started driving the ten miles to pick up Aubrey.

When I drove up his driveway I drove past the garage and up to the front door. As I started getting out Aubrey came around the corner with his conventional rod and fly rod. This gets me a little excited because he hasn't given up on fly-fishing.

When most people around you don't fly fish, it is difficult to continue especially when you don't really know all the ins and outs about the sport. Teaching yourself to fly fish is difficult and I am glad I can give him any pointers I can so he can hopefully continue learning the lost art of fly-fishing.

"Good morning, Aubrey. You ready to do some fishing?"

"I got to get something. I'll be right back."

He disappeared in the front door and returned carrying a mounted bass display. It was two very good-sized bass. One bass was chasing a perch and they were both attached to driftwood.

"Dang Aubrey. That looks good. You catch those?"

"Actually, I got the larger one but both bass was pulled out of the place we are going fishing this morning."

I sat up a little taller and chills ran down my spine.

"Well, let's get on the road and catch some more giant bass."

Once loaded up we took off driving to his grandpa's house. Since I didn't know the way Aubrey gave me directions.

Along the way, Aubrey talked about the honey hole and all the large fish he had caught.

"Did you get any of those large bass on your fly rod?

"No. Just my regular rods.

"Well maybe I can show you a little and that will help you land the next big one on your fly rod instead."

That would be the ultimate for me. Passing on a lost art of fly-fishing and my nephew catching trophy fish.

We pulled into Aubrey's grandpa's driveway. I drove up next to his grandpa's truck, turned the engine off, and we both got out of the truck. I glanced up and saw his grandpa coming out of his front door with his fishing gear.

"Good morning, how's it going?"

"Good morning, Andrew. Things are pretty good. You ready to do a little fishing?"

"Always."

As he walked up, I came in close for a hug. He really doesn't feel comfortable hugging, but I get a kick out of getting him out of his comfort zone.

"Come on now, get in here and give me a hug."

He reluctantly leaned in and gave me a small hug. I just smiled and chuckled to myself thinking one of these days he is probably going to punch me. Oh well, I guess I will keep on until that day comes.

SECRET HONEY HOLE

"Well boys, put your gear in the back of my truck and we'll take off."

"Yes sir."

We both grabbed our gear and placed it in the bed of his truck. Once our gear was loaded, I grabbed my sausage biscuit and coffee and jumped in his truck.

We were quickly on our way down the dirt road and headed toward the secret honey hole. I started daydreaming again imagining myself pulling in the largest bass I have ever caught one cast after another.

I was pulled out of my daydream with the sound of grandpa asking me something.

"What's that you got there. Biscuit? You are planning on eating that?"

"Well, that was the plan."

"Well, Aubrey's grandma is making breakfast for Aubrey and the both of us just so you know. You might want to just wait."

"I'll keep that in mind. Thanks for the tip."

A little further down the road I said,

"So, how's retirement treating you?"

Grandpa looked over with a very serious face and said,

"About as good as a baby treats its diaper. I'm busier now than I ever was while I was working."

I laughed and said,

"Well, I've got another five and a half years, and I can retire. Not sure if I'm going to but it is right around the corner."

I explained to him that my retirement plan is to retire in Vian area and hopefully start a fly-fishing store.

"I am sure the store will be more than just fly fishing but that is what I want to focus on. I will probably have to sell conventional fishing gear as well as hunting gear but nothing wrong with that. Maybe way down the road I will be able to have two different stores. One fly fishing and one conventional fishing."

He nodded his head as if saying,

"Good luck!"

During a lull in the conversation grandpa looked over at me and spoke.

"Andrew, I need you to take an oath."

I kind of got a little weirded out and didn't know where this conversation is going. I said,

"Okay?"

"You have to promise that you will never tell anyone where this fishing hole is, who took you there, and just know that I will deny any of it if it comes up."

I started to smile and realized that not just grandpa, but Aubrey who was sitting quietly in the back seat, were both looking at me in the most serious manner possible.

I quickly realized I had better make the oath and hope I still get to hit the fishing hole with them. I am sure they would have dropped me off on the side of the road had I not taken the oath right then and there.

"I swear I won't let the cat out of the bag."

(Do understand that I did not tell grandpa's name nor give any directions to the secret honey hole. I am hoping that the "Secret Honey Hole Fishing Police" don't stop by to place me under arrest, and I hope that Aubrey and Grandpa will still talk to me after writing this. Everyone say a prayer.)

THE LOST ART OF FISHING STORIES

As we pulled up next to the secret honey hole, I could see ripples from the fish eating on the surface of the water.

"I have to tell you I am incredibly excited. I hope this is as good as you tell me."

We all got out and went to the bed of the truck and put our fishing gear together.

I put Rufus together knowing that he would enjoy getting out and catching a few fish. As quietly as I could I looked over at Slim Jr. and said,

"Don't worry Slim Jr., I will get you out in a little while. I haven't really fished much with Rufus as of late, but I promise I will catch a couple of fish with you."

I glanced up hoping that Aubrey or grandpa didn't see me carrying on a conversation with my two fly rods because they would probably want to take me to the psych ward. I know it is strange but when you are usually fishing alone you need someone to share your experiences with and who better to share it with than your trusty fly rods.

Aubrey and grandpa were already walking to the edge of the water getting ready to get their lines wet.

"Okay Rufus, Let's get going."

SECRET HONEY HOLE

Rufus shook his head up and down agreeing saying,

"Yes. boss. Fishing time."

As we got to the edge of the water Aubrey had already gotten a small bass and threw him back in. This gives us hope.

Together Rufus and I cast the floating line and popper out as far as we could, let it land with a plop, and sit there for about ten seconds. We then start slowly popping the fly back toward us. This should get the bass excited and want to strike at the fly on the surface. Once we fully retrieved the line, we continued to toss the fly out as an offering to the bass for about 10 minutes with no bites or even lookers.

"Rufus, let's pull up and head down the shoreline."

As I glanced down the shoreline, I saw Aubrey again pull in a bass. Small, but at least a bass. This starts to get me a little discouraged. This isn't unusual for my trusty fly rods and me. We usually have problems fishing around other people. I am betting it is because the fish can since that there is someone watching me and they are thinking to themselves,

"Watch this. We can make this fly fisherman look like a total idiot. Just take whatever everyone else is throwing and don't even look at his fly. It will be hilarious."

THE LOST ART OF FISHING STORIES

I can just imagine them all gathered around a log just offshore, just like those punk kids at the mall who will stand at a corner and make fun of everyone else in the mall, laughing and carrying on watching the fool with a fly rod show his back side knowing that all he would like to do is do as well as everyone else around him.

Rufus and I walked the bank for about forty-five minutes and noticed that Aubrey and grandpa were standing at the truck, probably ready to go since they both were catching fish and got their fill. We did the long embarrassing walk back to the truck knowing that I looked like a fly fishing wanna be, fool.

As Rufus and I walked up Aubrey said,

"We're not getting much of anything. The fish don't seem to be biting at all. I only got three total."

Grandpa added,

"Usually by this time we have gotten our fill of large bass and are heading home. Let's go down to the other pond and see if we can do any better."

With a little of my pride restored, realizing that it wasn't just me, I quickly agreed saying in as calm a manner possible,

"Sounds great! Let's go!"

Pulling up to the next pond I was silently saying a prayer,

"God, please help me not look like a total fool. Let me catch at least one fish. You know how much I love to get skunked. I don't want to let Aubrey down. Please help!"

I got out of the truck grabbed Rufus and headed down to the water's edge. I glanced over just in time to see Aubrey grabbing his fly rod. I stopped walked over to see what he was using and helped him tie on a fly. I was very excited that he was going to give the fly rod a try even though his big Uncle couldn't get anything on his fly rod yet.

We both walked down to the water's edge and started casting out. I was ecstatic to see Aubrey land a small perch with his fly rod. Even though I haven't gotten anything, yet I was extremely happy for him. I walked around the water's edge a little further and started my casts again.

Within seconds of the fly hitting the water a fish exploded up and out of the water engulfing the fly in its mouth. With much excitement, I raised Rufus setting the hook deep in the mouth of the fish.

"Here we go Rufus!"

We both played the fish perfectly and landed the first fish of the day. A small and very aggressive sunfish. Not the giant bass I was hoping for but at least my prayer was answered. "NOT SKUNKED!!!!"

With the excitement of catching the fish Rufus and I quickly got the fly back out on the water. Within minutes again the fly popping on the surface induced another fish to attack furiously. This time I realized it was a little larger and a bass. Not the monster but at least another fish.

Rufus and I continued to catch small fish after small fish (6 in total). While fishing I noticed that Aubrey kept getting bites but no fish. I walked over and gave him some pointers and tied on a different fly. A popper. It seems to be working well for me so why not.

He also began to catch small fish with his popper. I glanced over and saw grandpa working the deeper edge of the pond and was pulling in larger bass and even huge crappie. I decided now was the time to go get Slim Jr. and try for some larger fish. Slim Jr. had his sinking line that would get the fly down a little further for those larger fish to eat.

My first long cast with a Wooley Bugger attached to the end of the line resulted in a decent sized crappie. I continued down the shoreline hoping for larger fish and finally was able to hook some decent sized bass and larger crappie.

I looked up to see grandpa watching saying,

SECRET HONEY HOLE

"Well, it's about that time."

"Good to go."

I kept my line going for a little longer and then Aubrey came over. I took this opportunity to help Aubrey with his casting and tried to show him a couple of things. After a couple of minutes, I noticed that grandpa was ready to go, and I quickly packed up and both Aubrey and I got in the truck.

If it were just Rufus, Slim Jr., and I we could have stayed all day long. I know that not everyone is enthusiastic about fishing as we are and that a couple of hours is usually good for most people. Oh well, nothing wrong with that. At least I got to hit the secret honey hole I have heard so much about. Although, we didn't catch the big bass we at least did catch quite a few fish. Well worth the trip.

On our way back to grandpa's house we talked about the fish we had caught and the amazement that the large bass just weren't interested.

"Not the worst fishing trip I have been on and any day fishing beats anything else."

About halfway back to the house grandpa again looks over with a very serious face and says,

"I noticed that you ate that biscuit."

"Yes sir."

"Let me give you a little piece of advice. When we get to the house you walk inside say hello to grandma then sit down and get ready to eat. You had better eat like you never had that biscuit. She has spent her morning fixing the breakfast and wants to know that you and Aubrey got the food necessary to carry on. I don't care if you are full or not. Just eat everything that she puts in front of you."

I smiled very big because I am very accustomed to this already. My wife's grandmother for every meal would fix huge dinners. There was more food there then I have ever seen at a dinner growing up. Appetizers, main meals, desserts, never ending desserts.

I was used to just eating the main course and that was it. In my house, there was hardly ever a traditional meal. Not that having the traditional meal was bad we just never really ate that way.

I would fix my plate at my wife's grandma's house and to my standards would be overfilled. Her grandma would always want to put more on my plate. Once I was finished that was it. I hardly ever had room for dessert or anything else, but I did notice that her grandma would be incredibly upset saying,

"Is that all you're going to eat? Is it bad? Was there something wrong?"

I would always be very courteous and explain I was not accustomed to eating that much and I had to let my food settle before being able to eat more.

Needless to say, I have gotten a little older and I have worked hard at stretching out my stomach to accommodate more and more food to ensure that everyone doesn't get offended, and I show them how much I like their food.

So, when we got to Aubrey's grandma and grandpa's house I came inside and gave my customary hugs and kisses and then did as I was advised and ate the delicious meal to the best of my ability. And yes, my ability is pretty good now.

After breakfast, we went downstairs and visited for a while and grandpa and grandma showed me all the trophy fish and game grandpa had killed over the years. I must say I was incredibly jealous. I am sure by the time I am his age I will hopefully have been as successful as him. I guess only time will tell.

To end the days fishing trip Aubrey and I went outside, and I showed him some different techniques that will hopefully help him in his strive to be a better fly fisherman. He is a good student, and it gets me incredibly excited to have someone to share my experience with.

THE LOST ART OF FISHING STORIES

There is nothing better than fishing with family and friends. Fishing by yourself is good but the shared experiences you have with family and friends is way better, even if you feel like you have no idea what you are doing and everyone else is doing great. At least you have a great story to tell, and you can always do what true fisherman do.

Embellish the story! ;-)

Story 6:
Words of Wisdom

My father in law, Bert ""Junior" Risley, after a rabbit hunt.

Words of Wisdom

Getting ready to head out the door, my father-in-law, Junior Risley, asked "Where 'ya you going fishing?"

"Was thinking down below the dam."

"You better be careful. When they let water out of the dam it rises pretty fast. You could easily get swept away."

I chuckled and thought to myself, I think I can handle myself. I'm not as old as you and a little stronger.

Of course, I wouldn't dare say that out loud and just said, "Ok Junior, I'll be careful."

I turned and headed out the door to start my day of fishing.

I had decided to go to a spot I hadn't tried fishing before and try things out there (of course, being the stubborn individual, I am I didn't let anyone know exactly where I was going). It was a wide part of the river, and the water only came up to about my knees. This would be a great spot to fish and just have a relaxing day battling trout up and down the river.

I put on my waders, grabbed Rufus, and headed out on the water. I did my usual tactic of starting my casting right next to the shore because many times the fish are very close to the edge relaxing and just shooting out to catch the nearby floating flies and nymphs in the faster current.

As Rufus and I made false casts preparing to let the fly into the perfect spot on the river we could see several fish jumping at different insects on the water. We cast and let my dry fly land peacefully on the water on the outside edge of the first seam. The perfect spot.

"Rufus, we still have it!"

The fly landed about ten feet upriver from a ring where a feeding trout had surfaced just moments before. The fly floated ever so effortlessly down the seam looking just like the other flies on the river.

"Rufus, if I were a trout I would definitely want to eat that fly. It looks perfect."

As the fly floated closer to the dissipating circle, I mended my line ensuring to keep the line as tight and straight as possible to better apply the "Hook Set" when needed.

As the fly floated, just before the last seen rising trout, you could cut the tension with a knife. All of a sudden, a burst of activity erupted from underneath the drifting fly. Neither Rufus nor I were tricked into setting the hook early. We allowed the trout to grasp the fly in his mouth, turn toward the pebbles on the bottom of the river with a splash, and swim underneath the surface of the water.

"Now, Rufus!"

I raised Rufus toward the sky allowing the line to come tight which turned the fly in the trout's mouth in order to hook him perfectly in the corner of his mouth. A perfect "Hook Set".

With almost professional precision Rufus and I were able to hook a fish on the first cast in a new spot on the river. I couldn't have been more pleased. We were able to fight the fish just as perfect as the "Hook Set" and within minutes landed the fish.

"Rufus, too bad we didn't have anyone here to film today's adventure."

Rufus in his normal joyous actions nodded his head up and down agreeing with everything I said. "Yes boss, totally agree boss."

After releasing the trout to fight another day, we worked our way across the river landing another three fish within twenty minutes. A perfect morning so far.

As Rufus and I worked our way upriver I realized that I must be working a deeper hole than we have worked up to this point and decided to walk back across the river to the more shallow area.

As we moved across the river, I realized that in fact it wasn't that the river itself didn't actually have just a deep hole, but this part of the river must just be deeper all the way across. I stopped and worked my way back down the river to the area I had originally started but the water there was deeper than when I started. In fact, the river seemed to be getting stronger and really running fast making my footing give way.

"Rufus, why didn't you tell me they were going to let water out of the dam?"

Rufus of course ignored me this time and didn't even nod his head one way or the other.

We had been so engrossed with what we were doing that we didn't hear the five horn blasts letting everyone know that indeed they were going to let water out of the dam and to get out before you get washed away.

Not knowing how long they would let water out of the dam Rufus, and I needed to get across the river back to our vehicle.

"Rufus, how could you let me be so naive as to not let someone know exactly where we were fishing? We could be in some pretty big trouble here."

Rufus just shook his head back and forth as if saying, "That's what you get for thinking you are better than someone else, even though his many years of life have taught him this life lesson already, or he wouldn't have told you about it before heading down here today."

Of course, I didn't want to hear Rufus rub my nose in my obvious mistake like you would a dog who has urinated on your carpet. So, I quickly headed across the river in order to get back to the truck.

I could feel the current getting stronger and stronger as we took each small step across the river. Each step felt like an agonizing reminder that in fact Junior, despite his seemingly simple ways has indeed learned a lot in his long life and I should heed his advice when he speaks instead of just acting like a know it all.

Rufus and I eventually made it across the river and had to make the journey back to Junior's house. Knowing that I would have to tell him he was right while my pride drifted down the river, passing by every fisherman telling them all what an idiot I had been.

Once back at Junior's house I gathered my things and went inside. I knew that I would be asked how everything went and was trying my best to prepare myself for the embarrassment I was going to suffer.

Looking back on this incident and not having him around any longer as he has now passed away just six short days ago, I realize how wise the man really was. He may not have had a college degree or had been a philosopher, but I now realize how smart he really was.

He has shown me things every day that I spent with him from how to fix my vehicles when there was trouble to how the small-town man looks at politics and how everyone should vote Republican. He was a man that didn't hold anything back and laid it all out on the table.

He wasn't afraid to tell you anything from "You sure have gotten fat" to "You better be careful. When they let water out of the dam it rises pretty fast. You could easily get swept away."

A wiser man is hard to find. Thank you, Junior, for your everlasting impression you left on me and allowing me to have your daughter as my wife. I will always love you and will strive to be the man that you were and will always be to everyone you met in your life. I love you.

Story 7:
Bamboo Heritage

The day my wife and I took Olga to Beaufort, NC.

Bamboo Heritage

Sitting on the couch with my wife Karleen she looks over and says, "The baby will be at the sitter tomorrow. Want to take a motorcycle ride?"

I, being the opportunist I am, jumped at the request as quickly as I could.

"Yes, Ma'am. Sounds good to me. Where would you like to ride?"

"Let's go to the little town we went to when we first got here. It was a really nice quiet town. There are also some things I would like to see."

"OK sounds good to me."

I quickly got up and headed toward the garage to do the normal pre-ride inspection on Olga, my faithful Russian Motorcycle with sidecar. My wife asked, "Where are you going?", as I had walked out of the room in the middle of a show we were watching on television.

I turned and said, "To make sure Olga is ready for our trip tomorrow."

"You can't wait until after the show?"

I turned around and said, in my best John Wayne accent, "Yes Mrs. Cox, whatever you say Mrs. Cox."

As I walked back to the couch, my wife was smiling widely saying, "Whatever Mr. Cox, Have a seat Mr. Cox."

I sat down like a good husband and watched the rest of the show.

Later that evening I went to do my inspection on Olga. As I checked the oil, I could only think about being out on the open road with the wind blowing across my face and the love of my life riding in the sidecar beside me.

We used to take many trips on Olga, but since we our sweet bundle of joy came in our life (baby Madison) we have not had the opportunity to go on many bike rides. I guess such is life with a child.

I finally finished up the inspection by putting air in the tires. I turned around to find my wife watching me from the garage door.

"Are we ready for tomorrow?"

"You bet. Just finished everything. Don't know about you but I am really excited."

We both went inside the house to go to bed for the evening. Unfortunately, the night just drug on and on. I think I woke up about ten times just wishing the next morning would hurry up and get here.

The next morning my alarm went off with a startling air raid sound (this isn't really out of the norm for me because this is one of the few sounds that actually will annoy me enough to roll over and get out of bed).

I jumped, thinking at first that the world was coming to an end but quickly realized I wasn't actually in a zombie movie fighting to keep order in the world. In a sigh of relief, I leaned over to shut off the alarm.

After lying in bed for a couple of minutes, trying to make more since of why my alarm was actually going off on a day off from work, I remembered that today was a day we get to take a ride on Olga to Beaufort, North Carolina. This was an awesome little town on the crystal coast of North Carolina that has many small shops and is a seaport village that will ferry people out to a reserve on an island where there are still wild horses running around (granted, not large horses but wild horses still the same).

I moved the dogs off my legs, their normal sleeping spot, and proceeded to drag myself out of bed. I went through the daily routine of getting ready then went to get Madison ready to go to the babysitters. Waking up Madison in the morning is one of the greatest things I have had the opportunity to do in my lifetime. She is always such a sweet baby in the mornings cooing and talking in that sweet little voice I have come to love so much.

I thought to myself how blessed Karleen and I are to have had this bundle of joy in our life. As I leaned over to wake her, she was sleeping in the peaceful baby sleeping position that you just know she is sleeping hard. You know the one! On her stomach, knees under her, with her butt up in the air!

I leaned over and woke her as peacefully as possible. As I got her dressed and ready for her big day of visiting the babysitter, she could just tell that she was going to have a good day and showed me how excited she was. She just made it incredibly easy to get her up and ready for the day.

Once she was ready, I woke Karleen up saying I was going to drop off Madison and I would be back in a little while to go on our joy ride to Beaufort. In her usual cheerful morning voice, she mumbled, "Fiaidnke adoco elakndnv adoioklskdfoe!" Luckily, I can understand her morning mumblings and knew she was trying to say, "Fine, just let me go back to sleep for a while!"

I leaned over and gave her the usual morning kiss and said, "I'll be back in a little while. It's going to be a good day. I love you!"

I loaded up Madison and we both drove in the truck to drop her off at the babysitter's house. On the drive over we did our usual driving tradition. This of course consists of singing along to whoever is on the radio. This time it just happens to be Alan Jackson singing his gospel songs. Of course, we were both singing right along with him in perfect harmony.

Well, at least singing along with him.

As I pull back into the driveway, I open the garage door where Olga sat waiting to be pulled out for our motorcycle ride.

Walking up to Olga I said, "Hey girl, you ready to go for a ride or what?"

Olga just set there not saying anything. "I know Olga, you're tired too. Let me pull you out into the sun and maybe that will get you excited and ready to head out on our ride. Then I'll go in and make sure Karleen is up and ready for the ride also."

As I pulled Olga backward out of the garage she started to moan and creak like older people do when they first get up in the morning. I laughed out loud and said, "I know you're tired. It will get better the more you move. It's always that initial movement that is the hardest. You'll be alright."

Olga, even though she is a 2010 model, still has that old motorcycle design and there isn't much on her that is actually considered newer. She has drum brakes (only 1 disc on the front tire), a boxer style engine that's air cooled, a bulletproof heavy transmission design, clunky shaft drive train, coil spring shock system, swing arm suspension on both motorcycle and sidecar, all on a double cradle frame. Old engineering that still works today.

Many people say that she is unreliable and just not a good motorcycle, but I believe that as long as you ride her, the way she was designed to ride, then there will be little problems. If there are problems then it is usually easy for anyone to be able to fix, instead of having to take her to a dealer and have only the techs be the only people that know how to work on her.

Once I pulled her out, I put her in neutral and prepped her for ignition. I decided to start her with the kick-start instead of the electric starter. This is one feature that everyone gets a kick out of (no pun intended). It only took me two tries and she fired right up. You could tell she wasn't really warm and ready to go right away like most newer bikes, but once she is given some time she will warm up and can go forever.

I let her run in the driveway for a while to ensure she was running correctly then turned her off to go check on Karleen. As I walked inside, I was surprised to find Karleen sitting in the living room dressed for the motorcycle ride.

"Wow, already dressed huh! You must be pretty excited."

"Of course, I am. It's been almost seven months since we were able to take a ride together."

"Well let's get outside and go on our little adventure."

We both grabbed our gear and headed out the door to load up Olga and head on down the road.

After loading Olga and dawning our riding gear, Karleen got in the sidecar, and I kicked over Olga's engine. This time she started on the first kick, and it didn't take long for her to start purring like a kitten.

We headed down the road on what we hoped would be "A Great Adventure". We drove through the neighborhood along all the base housing. When I tell people I live on Camp Lejeune, North Carolina they always look at me a little crazy, but it is actually pretty much like living in any small town in America with the exception that everyone living there is in the military.

The only other interesting thing is you can always hear explosions and gunfire pretty much every day. We always say that is the sound of freedom. The base itself has a grocery store, convenient stores, a small mall, boat docks, gyms, elementary, junior high, high school and even a college. There are also places for the Marines and families to hang out after work like the bowling alley, movie theater, and staff clubs. I guess you could say that living on base is pretty good. You rarely have to worry about illegal activities and for the most part it is a pretty safe environment.

We pull out of the front gate and head north toward Beaufort. Driving in North Carolina always reminds me of eastern Oklahoma. There are large groves of trees, green grass everywhere, and many fields for farming. I guess this is why I like being stationed here more than when we were in California. "Reminds me of home."

While riding down the road several cars pass us and as usual, they stare at my wife and me riding Olga. Many times, you can see the parents in the front seat pointing out the "old timey" bike to their children and the children jumping up to get a quick look, peering out of the back window and waving to see if they could get a reaction from the motorcycle rider. Of course, I always try to wave back as much as possible. I do enjoy the smiles on everyone's face as we drive by.

When riding the bike, I always picture myself like the character in the book, "Zen and the Art of Motorcycle Maintenance." In this book, the main character rides along while his mind seems to drift from topic to topic. When riding motorcycles, you can't really carry on many conversations, so you have to keep your mind occupied as you roll along. For me personally there is a lot of reflection on what is happening in my life and can at times solve many of my problems (or at least help me come up with a viable solution). It is a great way to just relax and reflect.

While riding through Swansboro, a small town near my house, we cross a bridge over one of the many bays. I can see many fishing boats and people fishing on the peer. I just imagine myself with my kayak floating in the current, fishing with my faithful fly rod Slim Jr., with his line in the water. This time of year, is perfect for catching sea trout. They are a great fighting fish and make's the fishing exciting.

As we pull into the small town of Beaufort, a small fishing village with many small antique shops and historic buildings, we notice there is another Ural Motorcycle parked across the street from where I was planning to park. I reached over and tapped Karleen on the shoulder and pointed over to the other Ural.

The new Ural was a black and red motorcycle that looked like it had been ridden quite a lot. It had street tires on it, which told me that the owner stayed on streets and didn't do much off roading. I immediately parked Olga and got prepared to venture over and meet the other Foil Head (a term that most Ural riders call each other).

As Karleen and I were disembarking Olga, I noticed across the street an older lady was already setting down her cup of coffee that she was sharing with the other patrons at the small coffee shop and heading our way. I knew that she had wanted to talk about Olga and share her adventures of her motorcycle.

Walking up she said, "We don't see too many Ural riders in these parts. It's always good to see fellow Foil Heads."

I laugh and say, "I think you are the second Ural rider I've seen this year. Good to know there are more riders around the area."

As I showed the new Foil Head rider Olga, my Russian motorcycle, she explained that the other Ural motorcycle was actually her husband's bike. As I glanced over, I saw an elderly gentleman making his way toward us. As he arrived, he commented, "I have always liked the color green on the Urals."

"Thanks, I'm kind of partial of it myself." As we sat and discussed our adventures on our respective motorcycles my wife had already ventured in and out of one of the antique shops and made her way back over to Olga, myself, and the other Foil Heads. I knew this was my queue to cut the conversation short and spend some quality time with the wife.

Finding a place in the conversation I, politely as possible, said, "Well, it sure has been nice meeting another Ural rider. Let's exchange information and we can get together for a ride sometime."

After exchanging information, I turned to Karleen and said, "Okay, now I am all yours."

She just smiled gave a little wink and with a giggle said, "Sure you are!"

We made our way down the street lined with antique shops, old buildings, and small diners. "First things first let's get some food." We stopped in a small diner that looked very quaint and sat ourselves. Not long after sitting a waiter came over to take our order.

He was a very cheerful waiter and was very thorough. He was able to raddle everything on the menu off to us without even taking a glance down. Any questions we were able to ask he would quickly raddle off the answer without hesitation.

Karleen ordered a coke, chicken strips, and fries. I ordered a coke, burger, and fries. Given that we hadn't really had anything to eat today this meal would definitely hit the spot.

After eating we headed out to start our shopping spree in the antique shops. I personally don't really like shopping in antique shops, but my wife loves it. I do know the types of things that she likes and can spot her dishes pretty quickly. I normally just walk around looking at everything and keeping my eyes peeled for anything that Karleen would want. Very rarely do I ever see anything that peeks my interest.

HOWEVER, on this particular day I ventured past a small fishing section. There were conventional rods and reels with old style lures that looked really cool. Since I am not really a conventional fisherman, I did my usual rummaging and taking in the beauty of how things were made in the past and the quality of craftsmanship but continued on to the next thing.

Then out of the corner of my eye I saw what appeared to be a broken-down fly rod. I of course had to take a closer look. It was partially buried behind the more popular conventional gear but sure enough there was a bamboo fly rod in a very old looking rod case. I had only seen things like this online and had never had the opportunity to see any old bamboo rods still in its original case.

This is something that sparked my interest and I just had to have it. I looked and noticed that the price was $70. I figured I had better show the expert and see if she thinks it would be worth the buy. As I started heading her way, I saw on one of the shelves, among the conventional reels, one lone fly reel. The reel had a two-way drag system and still had the old-style floating line attached. It was from about the same era as the bamboo fly rod. I would venture to say that whoever brought it in probably had them together at one point.

I quickly snatched the reel and brought it along. The price of the reel was $25. As I approached Karleen, she looked at me with a puzzled look on her face. She asked, "Are you alright? normally you wouldn't buy anything in an antique shop!"

I smiled and said, "I guess you are finally rubbing off on me."

"So, it only took seventeen years of marriage." We both chuckled and continued looking around.

After Karleen had said she thought it was a good buy, and we finished getting everything we wanted we gathered our things and went to the front to pay. When we got there, the lady commented, that the fly rod had been sold to her by a gentleman whose father was in the Korean War. He thought that is where the fly rod came from. He had no children to pass the rod onto and he himself had no interest in fly-fishing at all. This quickly sparked my interest and I wanted to learn more about the rod.

As we left the store, we walked over to Olga to put our new purchases in and then we continued walking the city streets.

After dropping off the new bamboo fly rod at Olga we continued our journey through the streets of Beaufort. We ventured in and out of antique shops, ma and pa shops, and even into a small museum. The entire walk around Beaufort all I could think about was the new bamboo fly rod and imagined how it came to rest in the small antique shop in Beaufort, North Carolina.

My imagination ran wild. I could just see a Marine during the Korean War getting some rest and relaxation. We will call him Anthony for now.

THE LOST ART OF FISHING STORIES

"Anthony" was a young Corporal of Marines who was part of 2d Marine Division. He was a squad leader and had led his Marines on many battles throughout Korea. He had been in Korea for going on 8 months and this was the first time he had gotten to go somewhere to relax.

It was a long and well-deserved break, and he couldn't wait to actually spend some time getting to do what he loved best, fly-fishing. He had led his Marines all over Korea and every time that he saw a lake or creek, he said to himself, "Too bad we aren't here on vacation. This would be a perfect place to get a fly rod and just have a couple hours of fun." In fact, most of his down time he would reflect on his day's back home fishing with his father and wished that someday he would live to pass it on to his children.

As soon as he made it to the town where he would spend his time relaxing and recuperating, he asked the other Marines if there was any place to actually go fishing. He asked everyone he saw in hopes that someone could point him in the right direction, and he would in fact get to really relax and recuperate.

While at the chow hall he finally got a good answer from a Marine he had just happened across that was discussing his last fishing trip at a small creek nearby.

Anthony asked the young Marine, "Where exactly is the creek and where can I get a good fly rod?"

BAMBOO HERITAGE

The young Marine looked up saying, "Corporal, there is an old Korean man just outside camp that makes fishing rods. I'm not sure if he has a fly rod but I'm sure he can at least tell you where to get one."

That afternoon, Anthony took off to hopefully have an adventure he had dreamed about for the last 8 months.

He walked down the small streets of the town looking for the rod maker. As he walked the streets, he was amazed that with the war so close to their town all the women and children just went along with their day as if nothing was actually going on just several hundred miles away.

He eventually came across a small shack that had several fishing rods leaning against the walls. Adrenaline from the excitement started coursing through his veins. Not the same adrenaline that he got while in battle but the excitement that came when he was a young child, and it was the first fishing trip of the summer with his dad. This was the only excitement that he wanted at this point and was so thankful that he was going to get to experience the feeling again.

He walked through the front door and saw a very short old Korean man in the back of the shop. As he approached the old man, he noticed that the man was bent over a workbench in the back. The old man was working on a fishing rod that was made of bamboo. Looking around he noticed that all the fishing rods were actually bamboo but no fly rods in sight.

Anthony continued to look around the old man's shop looking for a fly rod. Once the old man had finished putting the finishing touches on the fishing rod Anthony waited for the perfect opportunity and asked hoping he spoke English, "Excuse me sir, do you have any fly rods?"

The Korean man turned and looked at him and gave him a strange look. The man tried to say something in Korean to him, but Anthony couldn't understand him. The old man then walked over to the row of fishing poles and grabbed one saying in broken English, "This good rod! You buy?"

Anthony still looking around for a fly rod said, "No not that kind. Fly rod!"

The old man grabbed a different rod and said, "This better?"

Anthony, undetermined, continued looking around and noticed a bug flying around. "Fly rod!" and pointed to the flying bug.

The old man's eyes got really big and said in an excited voice, "Yes, yes, yes! Wait here!"

The old man disappeared through a door in the back and came back with a broken-down fly rod in a case. He was also holding a fly reel with floating line.

He held it up saying, "You want?"

Anthony almost shouted in joy but refrained himself and simply said, "Yes, Perfect!"

BAMBOO HERITAGE

The old man handed the fly rod and reel over to Anthony. Anthony took the fly rod and noticed that this rod was also bamboo. He immediately started taking it out of the case to inspect and see the new bamboo fly rod.

The fly rod had 4 different sections. The butt section, where the fly reel was attached, and then had two different sections with a tip. The first section with a tip was a little longer and heavier duty. The other two sections fit together to form a longer lighter section. It was designed to have two different sizes of rods without having to purchase two separate fly rods.

This was perfect and Anthony couldn't wait to get out on the water. He broke the rod back down and told the old man, "This is perfect. I'll take it!"

The old man got excited and quickly went back into the back room. He reappeared with a box of small flies that he had obviously made and another fly rod in hand.

Anthony reached into his pocket and pulled out money to give to the old man. The old man looked at the money and shook his head no and pointed at the bag that Anthony had on his back. Anthony thought to himself what would happen if he showed back up without his pack and decided that he could more than likely talk to his buddies and get another pack without anyone even knowing other than him, his buddy, and the fly on the wall.

Anthony took the pack off and got his gear out of the pack. Luckily the only thing he had in the pack was food and water for the day. The old man grabbed the pack and sat it under his workbench.

Anthony thanked the old man one more time and headed out of the shop. As he walked down the street, he heard the old man yelling, "Hey G.I., Hey G.I. wait." Anthony turned to see the old man running up behind him with the other fly rod in hand. "You want me take fishing?"

Anthony said, "Sure, let's go!"

The old man headed in a brisk walk toward the creek and Anthony followed quickly behind.

The old man and Anthony walked up to the creek and started putting together their fly rods. The old man moved much quicker and had his together waiting patiently for Anthony. It had been a long while since Anthony had done any fishing and he could feel his hands were incredibly clumsy.

Once he got his rod together the old man pointed to a small bend in the creek and told Anthony, "You go there. Be quiet. Fish scare."

Anthony nodded and headed toward the bend in the creek. Once he got close, he took out slack in the line preparing to make a cast. He noticed fish coming to the surface and knew they were hungry. He wound up and made several false casts. He could feel that each false cast was not how he remembered. "It has been a while."

He let the fly go and it landed with a little bit of a plop. He could see the fish scatter away from his fly. He thought to himself, "Calm down

Anthony, take your time and make a good cast." Letting himself regain his composure he tried again.

This time the fly landed a little softer and floated down the creek. No bites!

He tried again in the same area. Again, No bites!

He heard some commotion over his shoulder and looked over to see the old man fighting a fish. The old man's fly rod was bent over, and a large fish was on the other end of the line fighting for all it was worth. The old man just had a big smile and was slowly reeling in the fish. Once he landed the fish, he held up a good five-pound carp.

Anthony had never fished for carp with a fly rod and was amazed at the sight. He got excited and quickly got his fly back in action.

After casting for another thirty minutes and the old man catching another three fish, Anthony felt like he was getting the hang of casting again. He moved up the creek a little further and made a very smooth cast with an almost perfect landing of the fly.

He let it float down the creek for about four seconds and then BANG, a large carp smashed the fly and took it into its mouth and headed upriver as fast as possible. Anthony fought the fish perfectly. He thought to himself, "Just like riding a bike!"

Once he landed the fish the old man was standing close to him on the bank. The only statement to Anthony was, "Good fish."

Anthony found himself feeling just like he did when he was younger, back home, and his dad standing over him probably prouder of him catching the fish than he was of himself.

As I was deep in thought about where the bamboo fly rod came from, I realized my wife was talking to me.

"Here is the graveyard I wanted to see. These graves are really old, and it should be pretty cool."

"Sounds good sweetie."

We ventured into the graveyard and looked at all the different graves all the while I was still in my own thoughts about the bamboo fly rod.

After Karleen and I had our fill of Beaufort we headed back to Olga for our motorcycle ride home. We loaded all our new purchases in the trunk of the sidecar and mounted up for the hour-long ride home.

While riding I once again thought about Anthony and how he managed to get the bamboo fly rod home.

After Anthony's fishing trip with the old man he knew that he was ready to move on and finish his part in the war. He managed to get another pack, to replace the one he traded the bamboo fly rod for, from his buddy that worked in supply.

As he went on to his assignments in Korea with his squad, he carried that bamboo fly rod and could pull it out when times were tough to motivate himself and get back in the fight. He spent another six months in Korea before his unit was pulled and sent back to the United States.

When back in the states he took the bamboo fly rod fishing almost on a weekly basis. He took his father fishing and told his story of how he found the rod and the fishing trip he had while in Korea. He eventually married and had a child. Anthony knew that he wanted to teach his son about fishing and how it could help him in his life as well.

Anthony worked with his son year after year and was always the proud father. He was most proud of his son when for his fifteenth birthday he wanted to enter a fishing tournament. Anthony was so excited and headed down to enter his son in the tournament.

His son borrowed a boat from a friend and Anthony said he would be his driver for the tournament. Anthony watched as his son used his bamboo fly rod to skillfully fish for the large bass in the lake. He would cast toward the shore, utilizing a popper, and pop the fly back toward him with short bursts making a plopping sound on the surface of the water.

Without fail his son would get the bass all riled up and it was almost as if the bass were fighting over the fly that his son was providing. Bass after bass was pulled into the boat and collected for the tournament. Once the morning was over Anthony drove his son to the weigh station and his son had a total weight of thirty pounds.

There was no fisherman, conventional or fly, that even came close to his son's accomplishment. His son won first prize hands down. Anthony couldn't be prouder.

It was just one short year later that Anthony's wife and son were on a drive to town that would change his outlook on life.

As his wife and son were on the two-lane road they saw a car approaching fast from the rear. The car was driving erratically and shot out around their car. The driver of the other car realized that there was an oncoming vehicle in the other lane and tried to cut back in front of Anthony's wife's car. As he cut back in, he clipped their car causing it to swerve off the road hitting the curb and flipping several times before hitting a large oak tree.

When Anthony got the call that both his wife and son were killed, he was devastated. It took Anthony years to overcome the depression that ensued. He started drinking regularly and couldn't bring himself to ever pick up fishing again. The bamboo fly rod that had brought him and his son so much joy was now just a relic of the pain that now exists in his heart. "

While imagining the story behind my newly purchased bamboo fly rod the rest of the ride home felt like only minutes. As we pulled into the drive and into the garage Karleen looked over and said, "Thanks for the wonderful day. We should do this more often."

I looked over and said, "I couldn't agree more. I love you."

BAMBOO HERITAGE

We unloaded all our findings and went in the house. Now time to go pick up Madison from the babysitters.

When I got in my truck to go pick up Madison, I couldn't stop imagining the history of my new bamboo fly rod. I again thought about Anthony and how he lost his wife and son.

For years after the loss of his wife and son, Anthony drank the pain away. He didn't care for anything and only wanted his pain to end. One day while finally cleaning out his wife and son's things he found the bamboo fly rod. He remembered back, to acquiring the rod, and how much it meant to him and how he taught his son to fish with it. He decided to put the fly rod in the attic along with his wife's things to hopefully move on.

Five years later after extensive counseling and many hours, days, months, and years attending church regularly he was finally getting over his loss. In fact, it was in that very church that he eventually met his future wife.

They dated for several months and then went to the justice of the peace and were officially married. He found it difficult from time to adjust to having a wife again but with her support and love he was able to adapt and move forward. It was her love that allowed him to put most of the past behind him and gave him the ability to move on.

Eventu{||:}P"lobh [Sorry Folks, Baby Madison got in my lap and decided to type her own version of the story!]

Eventually, they had another child. A boy. Like most men that have had a loss he kept the boy away from his memories and kept his distance so he wouldn't get to close. His greatest fear was to suffer the same fate he did earlier in his life. It wasn't that he didn't love his boy, but he just found it difficult and wanted to shield his boy from the pain he had once had.

As the boy grew up, Anthony never took his son fishing. He always kept his past secret never talking about what happened while he was in Korea or how he and his first son did so much fishing. This was a part of his life that he would always keep to himself.

As Anthony grew old and was on his deathbed, he told his wife and son the story of his first family. Not as in depth as he probably should have but he just couldn't get it all out. He felt bad for not giving his all in the new relationship and wanted them to understand why he kept himself at bay and never spoke of what had happened.

Of course, his new family understood and still loved him unconditionally.

After Anthony had passed away his wife and son were going through the attic and found the bamboo fly rod. Not ever having any attachment to the bamboo rod and not understanding the history behind it the son just thought it was a fishing rod that he had from earlier in life. Since he didn't have a son that he could take fishing and not a fisherman himself he decided to take it to an antique shop in Beaufort, North Carolina to try and sell.

Well, of course this is where I found the fly rod and I will ensure that this story (no matter how imaginative it is) will pass along to anyone who will listen. So, in actuality you are the keeper of my imaginary story and I hope that you pass it on to someone else.

I don't exaggerate- I just remember big.

CHI CHI RODRIGUEZ

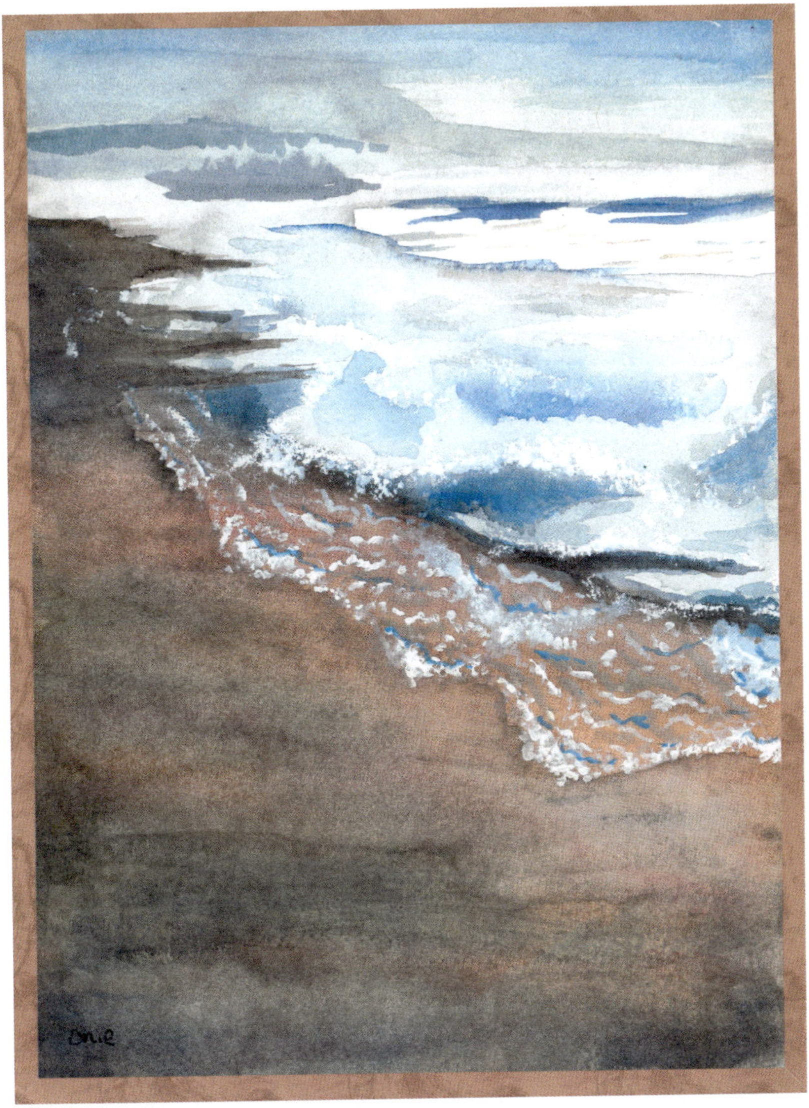

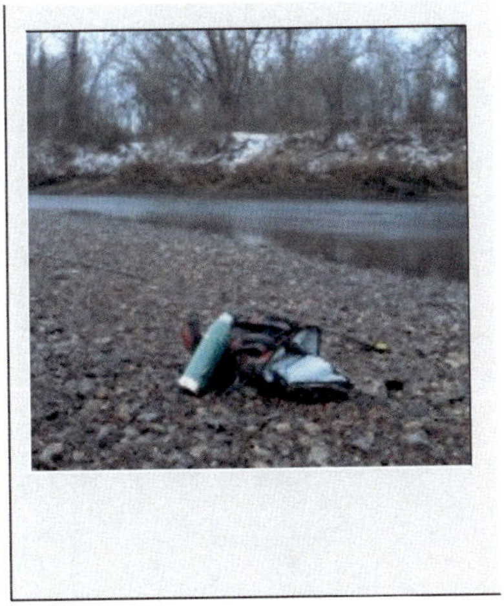

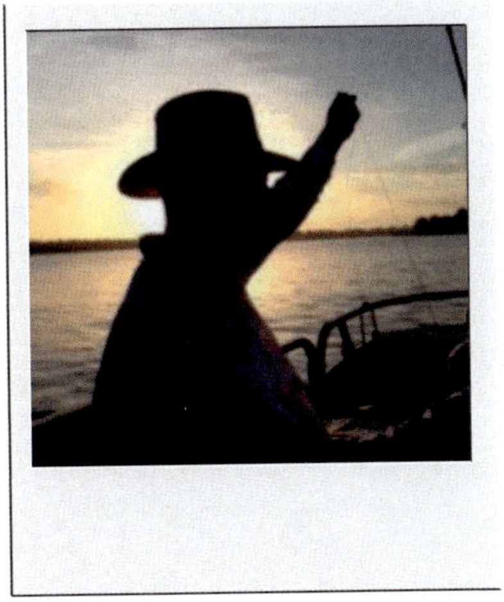

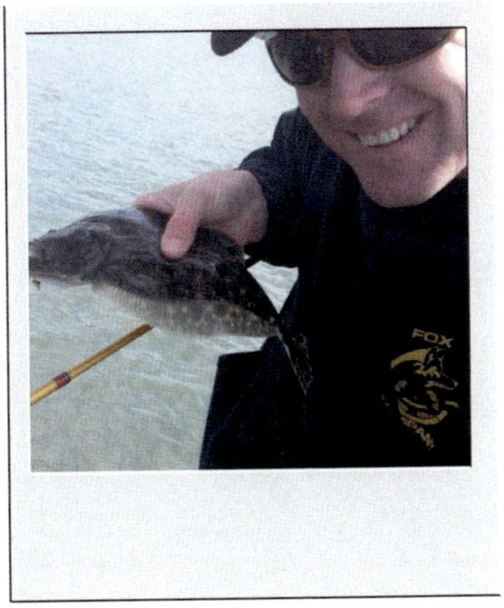
FOX

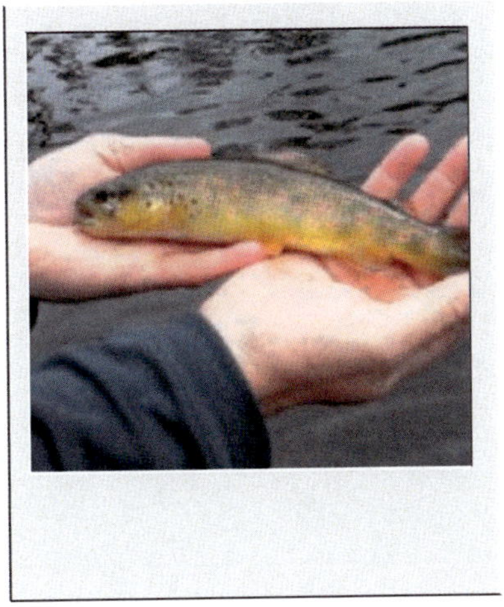

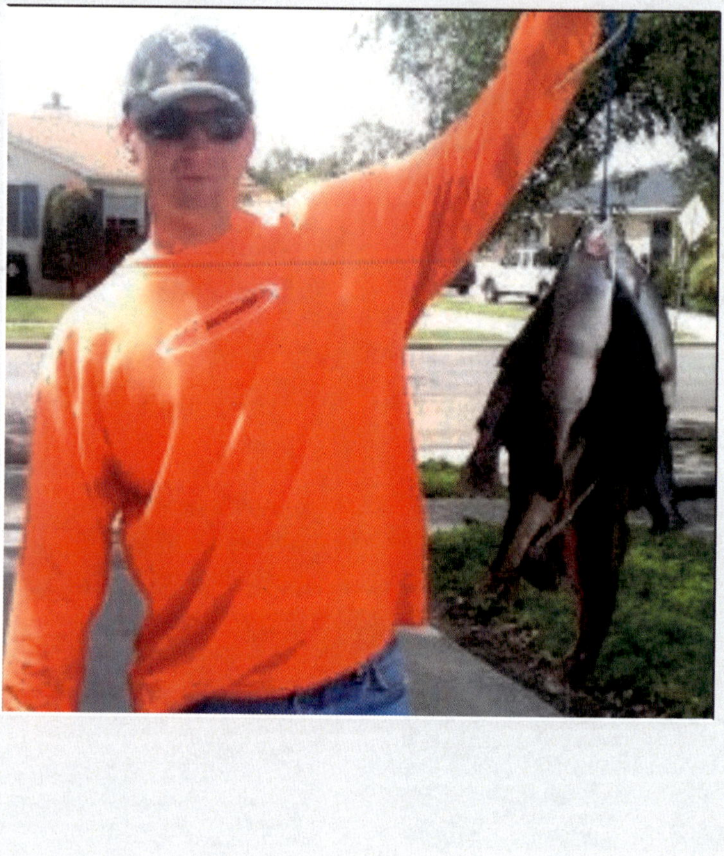

About the Author

Andrew Cox grew up in the small town of Vian, Oklahoma where he had plenty of family and friends to keep him busy. His parents, Leonard and Linda Cox, taught him Christian values and instilled in him a sense of pride in how he did every task. This pride has given him the ability to set his mind to something and not give up until it is achieved. He met his wife of over twenty seven years, Karleen Cox, in the 6th grade vowing to his mother that he would "marry that girl someday". After years of asking, she finally said yes. They were married and have been enjoying a blissful marriage ever since. Andrew and Karleen have been blessed with two beautiful daughters, Madison and Tayla who have given a new spirit to their family. Andrew joined the U.S. Marine Corps in 1999 which furthered his pride and values, teaching him to set goals and achieve them. Reaping the benefits of military life and achieving more than he ever thought possible he set his eyes on learning the art of fly fishing. With a little encouragement, he started writing about his experiences which brought him to the publication of this book.

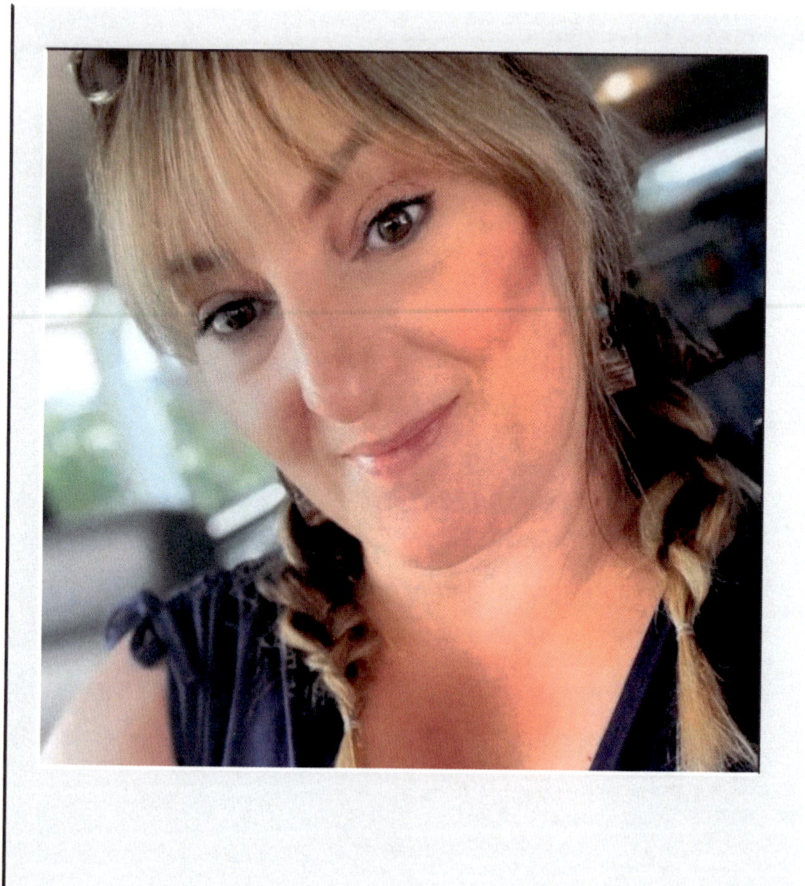

About the Illustrator

Onie "Virginia" Bailey is an artist/illustrator from Claflin, Kansas whose mediums are primarily watercolor, acrylic and mixed media. A hairstylist by trade, she enjoys bringing creativity into everything. Most recently, Virginia uses her art to create prophetic paintings, often painting live during worship services. Aside from being a worship leader at her church, her other creative outlets are singing, songwriting and playing guitar. Virginia has three adult daughters: Maya, Lydia and Amelia and one granddaughter Persephonie. Each one is beautifully creative in their own right. One of her favorite pastimes is gathering with her girls for painting days. Virginia aspires to write and illustrate her own children's books one day.

Fisherman's Prayer

God give me strength to catch a fish,
So big that even I,
When telling it afterwards,
Have no need to lie.

ANONYMOUS

Made in the USA
Middletown, DE
12 January 2024

47642937R00077